Hiya!

It's so exciting to be at the start of a brand-new series. The Lost & Found is all about a bunch of misfit friends who find themselves at the start of a very exciting journey! *Love From Lexie* tells us how it all begins . . . It's a story of friendship, first kisses and long-lost family, with a little library love mixed in for good measure. Lexie is such a cool character – she tries very hard to keep everyone else happy, but she's carrying her own painful secret inside. Not everything that's lost can be found again . . . and sometimes the things you're looking for turn out to be a lot closer than you think!

I hope you like Lexie's story. I've fallen in love with the Lost & Found kids and I can't wait to share stories from more of the characters as the series unfolds! Take time out to curl up and fall into a whole new world with Lexie and the Lost & Found!

Cathy Cassidy, x x x

Cathy Cassidy

LOVE FROM LEXIE

PUFFIN

PUFFIN BOOKS

UK | USA | Canada | Ireland | Australia
India | New Zealand | South Africa

Puffin Books is part of the Penguin Random House group of companies
whose addresses can be found at global.penguinrandomhouse.com.

www.penguin.co.uk
www.puffin.co.uk
www.ladybird.co.uk

First published 2017
This edition published 2018

001

Text copyright © Cathy Cassidy, 2017
Illustrations copyright © Erin Keen, 2017

The moral right of the author and illustrator has been asserted

Set in Baskerville MT Std
Typeset by Jouve (UK), Milton Keynes
Printed in Great Britain by Clays Ltd, St Ives plc

A CIP catalogue record for this book is available from the British Library

ISBN: 978–0–141–38512–9

All correspondence to:
Puffin Books
Penguin Random House Children's
80 Strand, London WC2R 0RL

Thanks . . .

Thanks to Liam, Cal, Cait and all of my fab family. Hugs to Helen, Fiona, Lal, Mel, Sheena, Jessie and all my lovely friends. Cheers to Ruth, my PA; Annie, who arranges my tours; Martyn, who sorts out the number stuff; and my fab agent Darley and his team. Thank you to Erin for the gorgeous artwork; to my lovely editors, Amanda and Carmen; and to Wendy, Mary-Jane, Tania, Roz, Ellen and all of the Puffin team for their help and support.

A special thank-you to the libraries I have loved so much and tried to save, especially Tile Hill and Earlsdon in Coventry and Sefton Park in Liverpool . . . and to many inspiring librarian friends who prove every day that the magic of libraries is alive and well and very much worth fighting for. Thanks to Cal and Jen for advice on the muso bits, and to Cait for letting me borrow the lyrics of her song 'Train of Thought'. Thank you to Mary Shelley the tortoise, for lending her name.

Most of all, thanks to YOU, my lovely readers, for making all the hard work worthwhile.

Cathy Cassidy xxx

The little girl is curled up on a second-hand sofa, snuggled in a handmade rainbow-striped jumper, her dark hair braided with bright cotton threads, an upturned library book at her feet. She is alone, hugging a knitted toy dog and watching *Frozen*.

Sometimes she pads into the kitchen to look at the clock on the wall. Sometimes she goes to the window and presses her cheek against the glass, looking up at the clear blue sky and then down to the pavement ten floors below.

She peels back the foil from a half-eaten Easter egg and nibbles it absently. When the movie finishes she goes to

I

check the clock once more, then returns to the window. The pavement glitters with broken glass and broken dreams, and when her eyes blur with tears she wipes them fiercely away with her sleeve.

She stays there, watching, waiting, until it gets dark.

1

How It All Began

Have you ever been lost? I have.

In a supermarket when I was a toddler; at a funfair, briefly, aged four or five; on a day trip to Glasgow when I was seven, in the crowds on Buchanan Street. Each time, I was scared, panicked. Each time, my mum found me, wiped my tears, hugged me tight, took my hand and made it all better.

I thought that was just the way things were, the way things always would be. If you were lost, your mum would find you and make things better. I took it for granted.

I didn't realize back then that not everything that gets lost can be found again.

*

I was nine years old when it happened, and I wish I could say I'd seen it coming, but I really didn't . . . I didn't have a clue. For starters, we didn't live a regular kind of life. We moved around a lot.

For a while we lived in a flat in Edinburgh, then a farmhouse in the Scottish borders, a cottage by the sea, and once, for a whole summer, in a bell tent.

We ended up in a high-rise block of flats on a Midlands estate, which was probably the worst place of all . . . but we were happy. Well, I thought we were.

The lifts smelled of sick and the pavements were starred with broken glass, but at last we had a proper flat with a TV and everything. There was no garden, but Mum said the sky belonged to us. We were on the tenth floor, so there was plenty of it.

'We could spread our wings and fly, Lexie,' she told me a few months after we moved in. 'Go anywhere! London, Brighton, the south of France . . . You pick!'

'We could stay here,' I said uncertainly, but Mum said that was boring. She took my hands and danced me around the flat, laughing, but after a while I pulled away, pressed

4

my nose against the windowpane and watched my breath blur and mist the glass. It was the Easter break and the sky was unexpectedly blue, spread out before me like a promise. I was weary of the moves by then, weary of endless new starts in new schools with new best friends who were never going to be forever friends.

'I'm not a staying-in-one-place kind of person!' Mum said.

'I think I might be,' I told her.

She ruffled my hair and told me not to be so silly, but she seemed anxious, doubtful. 'There's a whole wide world out there to explore,' she said, as if trying to convince herself. 'We'll get out there, the two of us, find new adventures! We'll find ourselves!'

I frowned. 'But . . . we're not lost,' I said.

'We are, Lexie,' Mum replied, and her eyes went all sad and faraway. 'We are.'

The next day Mum had an interview in town.

'I won't be too long,' she told me. 'A few hours at most – I might pop to the shops on my way back. You can watch a DVD while I'm gone.'

I slid *Frozen* into the DVD player and snuggled up on the sofa while Mum scribbled a shopping list on the back of an envelope. *Bread, milk, chocolate spread*, it said.

'I'll be back before it's finished,' she said, nodding towards the TV, and I barely looked up, just waved, my eyes still on the screen.

Mum went out just after 2 p.m. and she didn't come back.

Nina Lawlor,
Flat 7/10
St...

Dear Mum,

I waited as long as I could, but they came to get me in the end. I am staying with a foster family now but there are too many kids and I don't really like it. It is on Kenilworth Road but I forget the number because it fell off the door.

I am at a different school, the one near the park. Please come and find me soon. I miss you to the moon and back.

Love,

Lexie xxx

2

The Rescuer

That nine-year-old kid, the girl I used to be . . . she's just a distant memory now. She was brave and funny and fearless . . . but the thirteen-year-old me? Not so much. I fell to pieces and put myself together again, but things aren't quite the same.

Maybe I didn't get the pieces in the right places, because when I look in the mirror I see a girl I just don't recognize. If Mum came back, would she know me? It's a thought that worries me sometimes.

My mirror shows a pale-faced girl with brown eyes and freckles, her dark hair chopped into a short, angular bob. She smiles a lot, but her eyes are sad. Nobody has knitted her a rainbow-striped jumper for a very long time; nobody ever thinks of braiding her hair with cotton threads.

These days I live with foster parents called Mandy and Jon in a tree-lined street three miles away from the Skylark Estate. It's a nicer part of town, near the park, but I'd go back to the estate in a heartbeat if it meant having Mum back again.

I'm not sure that that will ever happen, but I will never give up hope. I'm grateful to Mandy and Jon, I really am, but they are strictly temporary.

'Of course, we don't know how long "temporary" will be,' Mandy had pointed out at the start. 'I know you don't want to be here, but how about we make your room feel more homey, more like yours? Pick out some bits and pieces?'

The bits and pieces I picked weren't quite what Mandy and Jon were expecting. I like to find the things that other people have lost, the stuff that they don't want any more – I like to keep it safe in case someone needs it.

My bed is draped in a charity-shop patchwork quilt; Mandy helped me to repair the holes, but I often wonder about the person who made that quilt. What was her story, and how did something made with so much love end up in a box with pink nylon curtains and a price tag of £2.99?

I found a red formica table in a skip at the end of the road, a wobbly chair that Jon had to treat for woodworm before I was allowed to paint it red with white polka dots, a bookcase I'd spotted at the tip. Most of the books on it come from charity shops or the library. A tambourine with ribbons and bells, an old felt beret with a vintage poodle brooch on it . . . they're all things that I've collected.

Once I found a box of old Ordnance Survey maps on the pavement outside a charity shop. The man in the shop told me to take them, that people had no use for maps in the age of satnav and Google Earth. I opened out the maps, studied the contour lines, traced a finger along rivers and coastlines. I tried to imagine what the places would look like: Mousehole, Prestwick, Polperro, Pontypridd . . . hundreds of towns and villages I'd never heard of. Mandy and Jon helped me to paste some of the maps up over the bedroom walls, a jigsaw of faraway places.

It's the perfect wallpaper for a girl who still has nightmares about getting lost. On those nights, I lie awake in the dark and wonder if Mum might have found her way to one of those faraway towns or villages and somehow forgotten to come home.

I had to switch primary schools when I moved in with Mandy and Jon, and though I didn't think I had the heart for building new friendships, I changed my mind when I met Happiness Akebe. She was a tiny, waif-like girl in an old-fashioned pinafore dress that hung down past her knees, and she was the only person there who looked more lost than I did.

'Call me Happi,' she said, holding out a hand for me to shake as if we were sharing a dorm in some posh 1920s boarding school and not just a slightly manic Year Five classroom.

'Are you?' I questioned her, fascinated. 'Happy?'

'I think I am,' she said with a grin, and her whole face lit up.

We were odd friends back then – the sad kid whose mum had abandoned her and the bright-eyed Nigerian girl whose dad was a super-strict church elder – but we understood each other somehow.

I knew I needed Happi in my life. I was still crying in my sleep, waking up every morning with a damp pillow and

11

an empty heart. Sometimes there were nightmares, visions of what might have happened to Mum; sometimes there were dreams of times gone by, and they were sadder still.

Mandy and Jon never complained if I woke up yelling or crying. They never made a fuss; they just worked around it, made allowances. Mandy would come in and sit with me, stroke my hair, whisper soft words, offer hugs. I never accepted those hugs; it felt like a kind of disloyalty to Mum, somehow.

At first, I struggled to fit in. I was used to being an only child, and Mandy and Jon had three other 'looked after' kids. There were two irritating little boys called Wayne and Brandon who were always yelling and fighting, and Bex, a terrifying twelve-year-old force of nature who decided to take me under her wing.

'What are you here for?' she demanded, that first day in foster. 'What's up with your parents? Drugs? Violence? Neglect?'

I blinked, terrified. 'I've lost my mum,' I tried to explain.

Bex looked exasperated. She was eating an apple, munching through the crisp, white flesh with a careless precision that fascinated me. Even then she was an impressive five feet ten inches of lean, pre-teen awesomeness, with turquoise-blue hair and a nose ring made of Indian silver. Her pink patent Doc Marten boots looked like they could crush any kind of snarky comment underfoot – maybe even crush you, if you weren't careful.

'Lost how?' she wanted to know. 'People don't just vanish. Did she die? Run away? Bang her head and lose her memory?'

'I . . . I don't think so,' I whispered. 'She just . . . went out one day and didn't come back. My social worker says they've reported her missing, but so far the police can't trace her.'

'Probably just wanted to be shot of you,' Brandon said with a smirk.

'Shut up, loser!' Bex snapped.

She chucked her apple core at his head, and it skimmed his ear, leaving a red mark and a smear of apple-juice slime. Brandon went off to Mandy to complain, wiping away tears of fury.

'You really don't know why she went away?' Bex asked. 'There was no warning, no trigger?'

Had there been? I'd thought about it a lot. Was it because I was boring? Because I didn't want to spread my wings

13

and fly, stick a pin in the map and choose a new place to live? These were the worries that poisoned my dreams – that it had been my fault. I'd learned to keep those thoughts to myself, though.

'Nothing I can think of,' I lied. 'Mum's a bit of a free spirit, but I don't think she'd deliberately leave me.'

Bex frowned. 'A mystery,' she declared. 'That's probably the worst possible thing, right? At least I know that I'm in care because my stepdad gets nasty when he's drunk and my mum is too useless to throw him out. And I can be a pain, sometimes. I like running away. Wayne and Brandon's mum just can't cope because she's got a new baby, what with the pair of them being horrible little yobs and all. No, your case is different, Lexie . . . a mystery. That must suck.'

I remember nodding, keen to hang on to any sympathy Bex might have going spare. I remember watching as her expression brightened, her eyes sparking with mischief.

'We'll turn detective!' she announced. 'Look for clues, unravel it all. Like Sherlock Holmes and his trusty sidekick, Watson!'

I could tell right away that Bex was going to be Sherlock and I was going to be Watson, but so what? Anything that might throw up a few clues about what had happened to Mum had to be worth a try.

'OK,' I told her. 'What do we have to do?'

Bex grinned. 'Elementary, my dear Watson,' she said.

LOST!

Mary Shelley has gone missing from the garden

of 67 Kenilworth Road. She likes cherries,

green beans and dandelion leaves, as well

as sunbathing, climbing and exploring.

REWARD of £5 offered for her return.

(Sorry, we're all a bit skint just now.)

3

Meeting Mary Shelley

The posters were everywhere, stuck on lamp posts, trees, fences, taped up in steamy shop windows. I was nine years old and there was nobody in the world more lost than me, but I stopped in my tracks and studied the posters. A lost tortoise from the student house along the road . . . a tortoise called Mary Shelley.

'This will be a perfect test case,' Bex told me. 'First we find the tortoise, then we find your mum!'

She took me to the local library, bigger and brighter than the one on the Skylark Estate I used to go to with Mum. The librarian, Miss Walker, was young and friendly, with candy-pink hair and polka-dot vintage dresses that swished as she moved. Bex told me that the missing tortoise Mary Shelley was named after an author of the same name – her book, *Frankenstein*, was about a mad scientist who made a monster from broken, leftover bits of people. I liked the idea of that – I was in the process of trying to put myself back together, after all.

I borrowed the book. The librarian told me to be careful in case it gave me nightmares, and I laughed . . . as if I didn't have nightmares every single night anyhow.

We borrowed a book on how to be a detective too, and on the way home we bought cheap notebooks from the corner shop and wrote the details from the poster inside. We found new cases – a lost scarf, a pair of mislaid school shoes that lit up when you walked, a stolen chocolate bar.

That last one was the only case we actually solved. The chocolate bar was mine – I'd left it on my bed and came back upstairs to find it gone. Brandon had brown smears all round his mouth and very sticky fingers, but by the time we found Mandy he'd wiped his face and swallowed the evidence.

Then, before I could find out if I had a talent for detective work, my social worker, Josie, stepped in and put a stop to it.

'Don't you think that some of these things might just be . . . well, lost?' she asked me, holding out the notebook. 'Tortoises do wander off. People lose things.'

'Lost things can be found,' I replied, stubbornly.

Josie raised an eyebrow. 'Is this what the letters are about?' she asked, and my cheeks burned because I didn't think anyone knew about the letters.

'What letters?' I bluffed, but I knew I'd been found out.

Josie sighed. 'The letters you've been sending to the flat where we found you,' she said. 'The place you used to live. Letters addressed to your mum. I understand why you might want to do that, but, Lexie . . . be realistic. If your mum comes back, she'll find you . . . but new people live at the flat now, and they're not happy about the letters.'

I blinked back tears. Why couldn't I send letters to the flat? How else was Mum supposed to know where I was when she came back? I'd promised to wait for her, and I had, right up until social services had taken me away.

'Lexie?'

My shoulders slumped. 'Whatever. I won't send any more letters to the flat.'

19

'Good girl,' Josie said. 'And we're all a bit worried about this detective thing . . . It's not healthy, Lexie.'

I can still remember the injustice of it. It hadn't even been my idea, but I was being punished for it. Not fair.

'Things have been hard for you,' Josie was saying. 'But the letters aren't helping. And all this detective stuff won't bring your mum back, you know that, Lexie, don't you? It's time to let go of the past.'

The tears I'd worked so hard to push away stung my eyes then, rolled down my cheeks like rain, but in the end I did let go of the past, just a little bit. Bex was bored with the whole detective thing within a couple of weeks, so we gave up. I was pretty sure that the light-up shoes had ended up in the bin, part of a vendetta between Wayne and Brandon, and the scarf had been found floating in the fish pond, culprit unknown. I still worried about the tortoise, though.

Time moved on. Wayne and Brandon went back to live with their mum, and Mandy and Jon told the social worker they'd like to make my temporary foster place more permanent. I wanted to tell them not to bother, that my

20

mum might come back for me any day now, but I knew they'd just look at me with pity in their eyes and I didn't want that.

I was practising handstands against the garage wall on the morning of my eleventh birthday when I saw it . . . a small grey tortoise, legging it across the lawn of 3 Kenilworth Road. Even upside down, I'd have known that tortoise anywhere. I ran across the grass, scooping her up as she rustled into the flowerbed.

'Mary Shelley!' I exclaimed, looking her in the eye, and I swear her scaly little mouth twitched a little as if she knew her name. 'Where have you been all this time?'

Upstairs, a window opened and Bex looked out. 'What're you doing? What have you got?' she called down.

'It's Mary Shelley!' I yelled. 'At last!'

Bex ran out and the two of us legged it along the street to the student house, me carrying Mary Shelley. I knew it was the right place because there was a one-wheeled bicycle upside down on the grass and a pair of skinny jeans hanging from an open upstairs window, dripping slightly. Bex rang the doorbell, and eventually a girl appeared.

'We've found your tortoise!' I said. 'Mary Shelley!'

21

The girl frowned. 'My name's not Mary, and we don't have a tortoise!' she said.

'No, no, the tortoise is Mary Shelley,' Bex explained. 'Don't you remember? She escaped a while ago. You put up posters offering a five-quid reward!'

'Is this a scam?' the girl wanted to know. 'Because I have no idea what you're talking about. We've only just moved in. And we don't have a tortoise!'

I blinked, and Mary Shelley blinked too, slowly and thoughtfully. She edged one front leg up against my collarbone and I noticed how warm her skin was, much warmer than you might think.

'It's not a scam,' I said.

'We do not have a tortoise,' the girl said, folding her arms. 'We do not want a tortoise. Last year's lot are all gone, and we don't have any forwarding address. Plus, there is no five-pound reward, no way . . .'

'Nice to meet you too,' Bex said, as the door slammed in our faces.

I sighed. It seemed kind of tragic that Mary Shelley should be found at last, only for her original owners to be lost. I spread a protective hand across her shell.

22

'They don't deserve her,' Bex said, as we walked back to the house. 'Ungrateful pigs. But on the upside . . . it's your birthday . . . Mandy and Jon have to let you keep her, right?'

Mary Shelley pottered around on the kitchen floor, sniffing politely at a cabbage leaf while we ate chocolate birthday cake and planned her future.

'We struggled to find a birthday present you'd really love,' Mandy commented. 'Now I know why . . . fate was taking care of things! She's lovely, Lexie!'

'I can keep her?' I checked. 'Really?'

'Of course!' Jon said. 'She'll be no trouble. I'd better check the garden fence so she doesn't go walkabout again . . . and according to Google she needs a heat lamp . . .'

I was so elated I could have hugged them, but I held back. I smiled politely at Mandy instead and she smiled back, a little sadly. I felt bad, but I didn't want them to get the wrong idea. We wouldn't be staying there much longer, not once Mum came back.

Meanwhile, though, Mary Shelley had landed on her feet, and I guess I had too.

Dear Mum,

My social worker, Josie, says the old flat has new people in it now, and they're fed up of me sending letters, so I am going to leave this in the park instead, on the bench we sometimes went to for winter picnics. If you happen to be there, maybe you'll find it, and then you will find me because the park is quite near where my foster family live. I don't hate it quite so much any more, and my foster sister Bex is nowhere near as scary as I thought. Jon put a new number on the door, so it's easier to find. 3 Kenilworth Road, in case you didn't get my other letters. I miss you loads.

Love,

Lexie x

4

The Misfits

These days, although Bex Murray is still fierce and full-on, I have learned to love her. She's like the eccentric and slightly savage older sister I never had.

Right now she is lying on my bedroom carpet with her legs up against the wall at a ninety-degree angle, her tartan-print Docs scuffing my jigsaw-map wallpaper a little. She says this is yoga, but I am not so sure, partly because she is simultaneously reading an English Lit textbook and listening to retro punk through her headphones. The Clash, it sounds like.

Bex is in Year Ten now. Mandy got her into yoga and Jon bought her a bass guitar for Christmas. Whenever she gets bad-tempered or cross she either hammers the bass

25

guitar on full blast for a couple of hours or morphs into Tree Pose, wobbling slightly on one leg.

As for me, I'm in Year Eight, and people have mostly stopped giving me those wary, wide-eyed looks that mean they think I'm acting weird. I fly under the radar, pass unnoticed: a quiet, bookish girl, a little bit serious but always willing to help someone in trouble. Bex and Happi are my trusty sidekicks – we're misfits, the lot of us, but so what? In a world of mixed-up, messed-up, broken jigsaw pieces, we fit together, and that's kind of awesome.

We see each other every day at school, and Happi comes over most Saturdays too. As if on cue, the doorbell rings and I run down the stairs to answer it. Happi is on the doorstep, clutching a cake tin.

'You told me to come over,' she says. 'A plan, you said. A big plan. So here I am . . . and I have cupcakes. Can I come in?'

'Always,' I say, holding the door wide. 'We're up in my room . . .'

I grab glasses and cold orange juice from the kitchen and head upstairs after Happi, who settles herself cross-legged next to the bed, feeding strawberries to Mary Shelley.

26

Happi is still tiny and waif-like. Her passions are maths and baking and the violin. Her parents are strict; they won't let her wear make-up or cool clothes, and she goes along with this. She is not a rebel – she's actually full-on geek, and very religious. None of these things are really plus points at our school, but somehow Happi has escaped being bullied. It might be because she's usually with me and Bex, but I think it's also because she's beautiful in a dramatic, ethereal way. Loveliness just shines out of her.

As misfits go, we are the lucky ones. Every single day I see tons of kids who are lost and struggling. The awkward, overweight girl from my English class who sits at a table on her own in the canteen every lunchtime and never seems to have any friends; the scruffy, sandy-haired new boy who joined Year Eight last September but hasn't quite found his feet; the pretty Year Eleven girl who always looks lonely. Millford Park is misfit central – there are sad kids, mad kids, bad kids, bullied kids . . . every variety of troubled teen you might think of.

What if there's a way to bring them all together?

'So,' Happi says with a grin. 'C'mon, Lexie. You said you had a secret plan . . . spill!'

Bex swings her legs down and helps herself to a cake and orange juice. 'Secret plan?' she echoes. 'Nobody told me! I thought we were just hanging out, drinking orange juice and eating cupcakes . . .'

'It's nothing major,' I tell them, although it is kind of major to me. 'I had a thought, and I wanted to run it past you, because Mary Shelley is being her usual inscrutable self and won't give me an opinion. I was thinking about us, and how lucky we were to find each other . . .'

'Lucky?' Bex scoffs. 'I've been trying to shake you two off since forever. Don't mind the tortoise, though.'

'I'm trying to be serious here!' I say. 'We are lucky, and you know it, Bex. If the three of us had never met, you'd still be a borderline juvenile delinquent, scaring the teachers and terrifying the kids and running away every couple of weeks.'

'I still scare the teachers,' she argues, an edge of pride in her voice.

'I'd still be crying the whole time and making my counsellor tear his hair out,' I push on. 'Instead of which I don't need counselling any more, and I haven't cried since

28

you made me watch that DVD of *Watership Down* on Happi's birthday.'

'You're still quite sensitive,' Happi tells me. 'That's a good thing, though.'

'She says sensitive; I say weird,' Bex chips in. 'Don't deny it!'

I shrug. 'I'm not denying anything,' I say. 'I'm weird and proud. The point is, I'm nowhere near as lost and sad as I was. Bex, you're loads better too and, Happi, you're just awesome, getting top grades in every subject and being a total violin genius . . .'

'Genius might be pushing it,' she argues.

'No, you are,' I insist. 'You're better than the teacher, I reckon. Look, there are loads of things I'd never have done if it hadn't been for you two, and that's down to the power of friendship. Right?'

'Right,' Happi agrees. 'With friends we're better, aren't we? You can be yourself, without feeling judged or laughed at!'

'You're nuts, the pair of you,' Bex scoffs, but I can see two telltale spots of pink in her cheeks. 'Good job you've got me to look out for you, that's all I can say.'

I laugh. 'Fair enough. But what about all the people who don't have good friends? Don't fit in?'

She rolls her eyes. 'Here we go,' she says. 'Please tell me this isn't some mad plan to rescue the waifs and strays of Millford Park Academy! Seriously, Lexie. No.'

I try to look wide-eyed and innocent.

'It's just . . . think about all those awkward kids, outsider kids . . . ones who are messed up, mixed up. Feeling lost and alone, getting into trouble even, when actually they just need to connect. We all know kids like that! C'mon, Bex! They're the kids who have nowhere to go, nobody to talk to. They're the kids we used to be . . .'

Bex leans over, squeezes my hand. 'Hey,' she says. 'I know what you're saying. But you can't rescue everybody, Lexie, the way you did Mary Shelley. The teachers should be sorting out the misfit kids!'

'Like they did with us?' I ask, and Bex sighs.

The truth is that the teachers at Millford Park are stressed and overworked. They try to look out for kids who are struggling, but mostly those kids fall through the net and stay lost.

Mary Shelley crawls up on to my lap, and Bex and Happi look at each other and sigh.

'It's a whole new concept,' I explain. 'A group that brings together the misfits, makes them strong and cool and awesome. Like a club where being odd or lost or misunderstood is the only requirement for joining. I even came up with a name – the Lost & Found.'

Happi nods. 'It could work, I suppose . . .'

Bex pulls a face. 'I'm not convinced that bringing all the odd kids together will magically result in some kind of huge happy-clappy friendship gang,' she says. 'It could be dangerous, like inviting the lions and hyenas to hang out with the gazelles. I mean, seriously . . . you'd be asking for trouble.'

My shoulders slump, and Bex shakes her head, exasperated.

'I have a feeling I'm going to regret this,' she says. 'Still, I can see what you're trying to do, Lexie. I'll help if you need me to.'

Hope fizzes through my veins, and I grin at my friends, hugging Mary Shelley close.

'I'm going to make a poster,' I say, stroking her shell. 'I'll put it up at school. I've already asked Miss Walker at Bridge Street Library if I can use the meeting room, and she said we could have it for free.'

The three of us spend a lot of time at Bridge Street Library – our school library closed unexpectedly over the summer break, the fiction books shipped out to make room for more computers. Miss Walker helped to set up the YA fiction reading group Happi, Bex and I are a part of.

People from the council have been lurking about a bit lately, sizing up Bridge Street Library and holding consultation meetings to see how much people care about the place. The meetings have been packed, according to Miss Walker, and the general opinion is that people want the library to stay just the way it is. The place is always buzzing, so I reckon it's safe, but if holding my Lost & Found meetings there helps even a bit, I'm happy. Plus, the lovely Miss Walker has promised to let me bring cake and make hot chocolate.

I kiss Mary Shelley's wizened nose and put her down on the floor before taking an especially battered old map of North Wales from the pile in the corner. I spread it out across the bedroom floor and Bex helps me to chop out a large rectangle while Happi fetches black ink and a couple of brushes from my desk.

I pick up a paintbrush, dip it into the ink and begin to write in big, wobbly letters, all across the Snowdonia National Park.

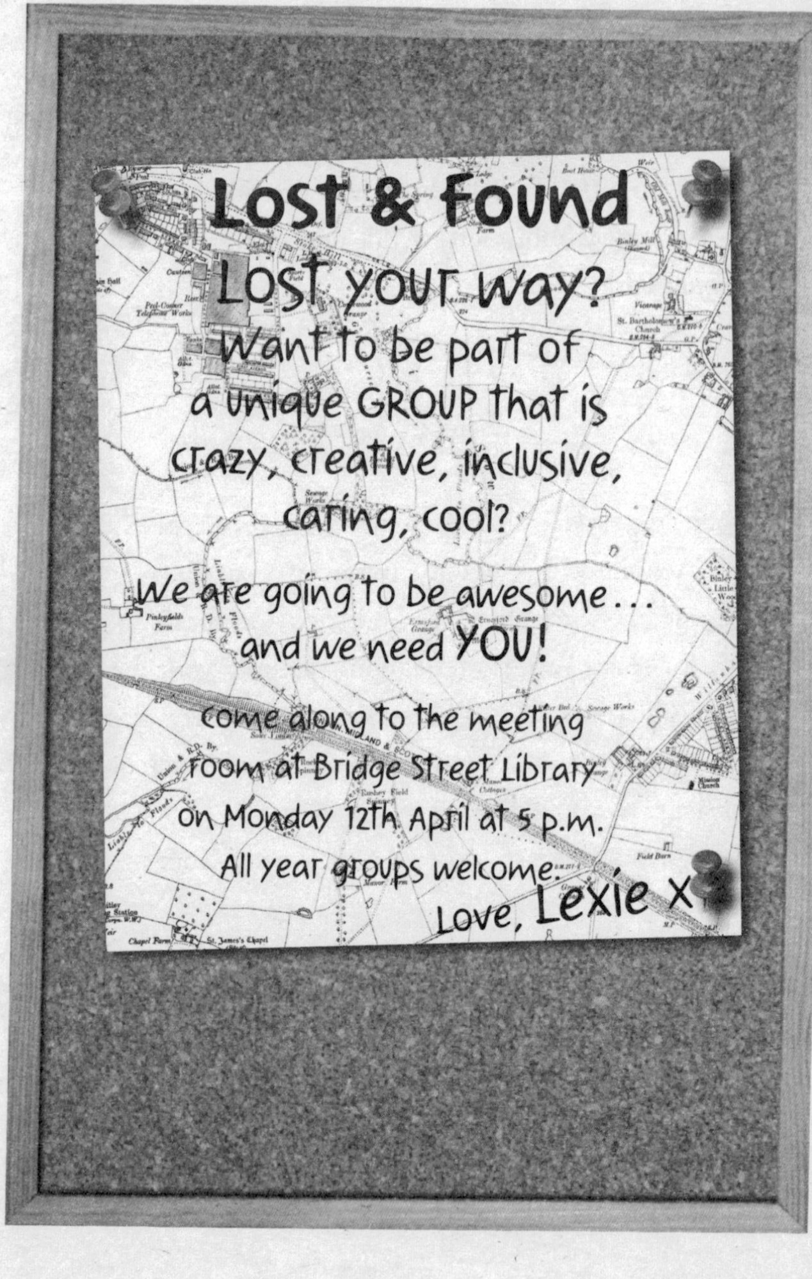
Lost & Found
Lost your way?
Want to be part of
a unique GROUP that is
crazy, creative, inclusive,
caring, cool?
We are going to be awesome . . .
and we need YOU!
Come along to the meeting
room at Bridge Street Library
on Monday 12th April at 5 p.m.
All year groups welcome.
Love, Lexie x

5

Poster Girl

Nobody pays much attention to the noticeboard at Millford Park Academy. It's enemy territory – a place where announcements about clubs and trips and sports fixtures jostle for space with posters about cleaning your teeth or calling Childline. Most kids swarm past as they cross the foyer on the way to lessons, a stormy sea of black blazers and stripy ties pulled dangerously askew.

It's breaktime now and I take the poster from my bag, unroll the rectangle of Ordnance Survey map and smile at the wobbly handpainted words. I have just pinned one corner to the noticeboard when an ear-splitting yell curdles the air. I whirl round to see two boys circling each other warily, a small crowd gathering in case something kicks off. One of the boys is tall, a Year Eleven maybe; the other is smaller, an infamous Year Nine kid called Marley Hayes. His younger brother, Dylan, was in my class when I switched primary schools; he still pops up in some of my classes now. Dylan's OK, but his brother is most definitely trouble.

I bite my lip, watching warily to see what he'll do.

The older kid seems to be taunting, teasing, because suddenly Marley launches himself forward, shoving the other boy backwards. The two of them are on the ground, wrestling and grunting; the air crackles with swear words and threats. More kids appear, screening the fighters from view, but I hear a crunching sound as an especially powerful punch hits home, a muffled whimper, the sound of ripping cloth.

'Quick, Simpson's coming!' someone hisses. 'Run!'

The foyer empties in a blink. Kids stampede in assorted directions until the space is deserted except for me, my poster and Marley Hayes. It's pretty clear that Marley has taken a beating. He struggles to his feet and takes a few faltering steps towards me, dazed. Another few steps and

36

I notice the tear in his shirt sleeve, the thin rivulet of blood that seeps from his nose.

Even in this shell-shocked and damaged state, Marley has something about him, a bad-boy aura that has lots of my classmates in thrall. His messy brown fringe and piercing blue eyes just add to the appeal. He stumbles to a halt beside me, resting a hand against the noticeboard to steady himself.

Mr Simpson the head teacher strides into the foyer, and I remind myself that rescue missions are not just for runaway tortoises and boxes of old maps and sheet music. I take a clean tissue from my pocket and hand it to Marley, who grabs it to staunch the nosebleed, wiping the evidence away.

'What's going on?' Mr Simpson roars, his voice echoing around the foyer. 'Has someone been fighting?'

His eyes fix on us, and I grab the poster and shove it at Marley to hide his ripped sleeve and rumpled shirt, which seems to have a muddy footprint on it.

'No, sir,' I reply. 'No fighting. It's . . . just us.'

'I definitely heard something,' the head teacher growls. 'No noise? No trouble?'

'Didn't see a thing, sir,' I say, shrugging.

He scans about, looking for clues. There are plenty – a small splash of blood on the dark lino floor, a lost shirt button, Marley's rucksack hidden behind a bedraggled potted palm. It hardly takes a trained detective to spot these things and put the evidence together; Mr Simpson doesn't manage it.

'What are you up to, Hayes?' he demands. 'No good, I expect!'

Marley coughs into the borrowed tissue and shows Mr Simpson the poster. 'I'm just . . . helping with this,' he says in a muffled voice. 'Not a crime, is it?'

Mr Simpson grits his teeth. 'Not a crime, no,' he says. 'And that makes quite a change for you, Hayes. What exactly are you doing with that handkerchief? Got something to hide?'

'Got a cold, sir,' Marley snuffles.

The head teacher rolls his eyes, exasperated, and glances at me. 'This young man isn't bothering you, I hope? Lexie, isn't it?'

'Yes, sir,' I reply. 'And no, sir, he's not bothering me. He's helping.'

'First time for everything, I suppose,' Mr Simpson mutters. 'Well, put your poster up and get outside. There's five minutes left of break. Bit of fresh air will do you both good.'

'Yes, sir,' we say in unison, as he stalks away.

The minute he's out of sight, Marley slumps. He stuffs the tissue, now streaked with blood, into a trouser pocket, but the nosebleed seems to have stopped.

'Thanks,' he says. 'Seriously. What made you do that? Stick up for me?'

I shrug. At times like this, telling the truth is the best option, so I do. 'You looked like you needed rescuing.'

Marley grins, then winces. 'Rescuing? Yeah, maybe I do. *Ouch* . . . that loser kicked me in the ribs!'

'Looks like he kicked you everywhere,' I comment. 'You're a bit of a mess. Better go see the school nurse.'

'Nah,' he says. 'Thanks anyway . . . Lexie, right? I'll live.'

He looks down at the poster still hiding his ripped sleeve and footprinted shirt, perplexed. 'What is this, anyway? *Lost & Found?* What's it about?'

I grin. 'Well, it's going to be a group, sort of –'

'A group?' Marley interrupts. 'Cool! Yeah, definitely! This place needs something like that! I'll come along, no worries!'

39

My eyebrows shoot up, surprised. 'Will you? Brilliant!'

'At the library?' he checks, studying the poster. 'Bridge Street Library?'

'It needs to be off school premises,' I explain. 'So we can all relax and be ourselves without the teachers trying to get involved. It gives us a bit more freedom.'

'Freedom . . . sure,' he says. 'And they won't mind the noise?'

'Noise? I don't think that'll be a problem,' I say. 'Miss Walker the librarian said we can use the meeting room. She's cool with it.'

'Great!' he says. 'We'll liven the place up a bit, I guess!'

Marley is grinning at me, his face alight with enthusiasm. Those blue eyes flash with energy and, though I can see a darkness behind it, I find myself drawn in. Marley is clearly bad news, but the lost and lonely come in all guises and if he wants to come along to my misfits meeting, I am not about to argue. Let's just say I'm starting to understand just what the Year Eight girls see in him.

'I play guitar,' Marley says, out of nowhere. 'Electric-acoustic . . .'

'OK . . . That's nice,' I answer politely.

40

'How about you?' he demands.

'How about me, what?'

'Musical instrument,' he says. 'What d'you play?'

'Er . . . tambourine, maybe?' I offer. 'I've got one at home, but I'm actually not very musical . . .'

Marley rakes a hand through his tousled fringe and laughs. 'Not musical? Ha! You're cool, Lexie! I like your style!'

I think I might be blushing. It's probably more of a pink glow than full-on tomato red, but still. Marley Hayes thinks I'm cool, and he likes my style. I think he's joking, obviously, but a compliment is a compliment, right?

'Why were you fighting just now?' I manage to ask. 'What happened?'

Marley tilts his chin. 'No big deal,' he tells me. 'I was dating his sister until last week, but it didn't work out. He wanted me to know he was not happy – well, I got the message. Sadly, he was bigger than me . . .'

'One of the Year Elevens?' I ask.

'Exactly,' Marley concedes, examining the footprint on his shirt. 'Size elevens too, by the look of it. I seem to have a knack for finding trouble.'

41

'You do,' I agree. 'That's what everyone says, anyway.'

Marley frowns at me like he cannot work me out at all, and I bite my tongue hard so I don't say anything else tactless or stupid. Talking to Mary Shelley is never this stressful.

'Anyway,' he is saying, 'this group thing . . . great idea, Lexie. I'll spread the word. Tell my friends. And my brother. He might be into it too.' Marley pins the poster up on the noticeboard, in a much more obvious place than I'd put it before. 'See you next Monday!'

He picks up his rucksack and walks away, whistling, only limping a little.

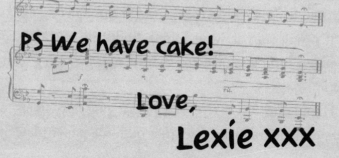

WELCOME TO THE FIRST MEETING OF THE LOST & FOUND GROUP!

Starting at 5 p.m. sharp!

Don't be nervous –
come in and we
can all get to know
each other.

PS We have cake!

Love,

Lexie xxx

6

The Group

I tape the new sign on the meeting-room door then go inside to arrange the chairs in a circle. Miss Walker comes in with a jug of orange squash, her polka-dot 1950s dress swishing.

'It's a lovely idea, this,' she says. 'Good luck with it, Lexie. Just give me a shout if you need anything! When people start arriving, I'll send them straight through . . .'

If people start arriving, I think. Suddenly, my bright idea seems a little less brilliant than it did, but I try to stay optimistic.

Happi and Bex arrive, Happi bringing fairy lights and home-made traybake. I set that out on a paper plate and

plug in the fairy lights. Bex looks doubtful. She wrinkles her nose at the cake and the lights, but she won't say anything to hurt Happi's feelings. She won't come right out and tell me she thinks the whole idea is stupid, either, even though I know she does.

'Reckon anyone will come?' she asks. 'I mean . . . did anyone actually see your poster? You know what the Millford kids are like. And if they did see it, will they understand what it was actually about?'

'Marley Hayes told me he'd come,' I argue, 'and bring his brother, Dylan. And mention it to his friends . . .'

'The Bob Brothers?' Bex scoffs. 'Why would they come? Marley's not a lost boy – he's a liability! I think he was winding you up, Lexie . . . well, I hope he was!'

'We'll see, I guess,' I answer, a little deflated.

'Let's be positive,' Happi cuts in. 'I mentioned it to Romy Thomas, that girl who sits on her own in the canteen. We're in orchestra together. Plus, there's a kid from school out there in the library right now . . . I bet you anything he's here for this. He looked really nervous!'

'OK . . . I'll go and see!'

45

Out in the main library, I spot the boy Happi mentioned straight away – it's the new kid in Year Eight, the scruffy, sandy-haired boy who hasn't quite found his friendship group yet. He's wearing a rumpled jacket and a faintly shifty look.

'Are you here for the meeting?' I ask.

'No, no, just getting a few books,' he mutters awkwardly, pulling the nearest hardback off the shelf in front of him. It's called *Surviving the Menopause*, and when he spots this he flushes a kind of crimson colour. 'Not this one,' he says, stuffing it back on the shelf. 'Obviously . . .'

'Obviously,' I agree. 'You're definitely not here for the Lost & Found meeting? It's in that room over there. We've got cake. I mean, even if you're not here for that, maybe you could just come in for a while? You'd be doing me a favour, really. I'm worried not many people will come.'

'Well, I did see the poster,' he admits with a shrug. 'It looked . . . interesting. If I was into that sort of thing, I mean. Cake, you say?'

By five o'clock, my heart is in my boots. Apart from Happi, Bex and me, it looks like the only people attending the first meeting of the Lost & Found group are Romy Thomas, the loner girl who goes to orchestra with Happi,

 46

and Jake Cooke, the sandy-haired boy I dragged in from the library. Both are silent, gloomy, checking their mobiles and looking very uncomfortable.

'Should we start?' Happi asks, and when I mumble something about giving it five more minutes in case of latecomers Bex shoots me a pitying look.

I glance down at my list of ice-breaker questions to get things moving, but the questions look feeble and awkward in the cold light of day. My mouth is dry. I wish I'd never thought of this in the first place.

Suddenly there's a rumble of raised voices and rattling, crashing, booming sounds in the library. I can hear Miss Walker squeaking something that sounds suspiciously like, 'You can't bring all that in here!' but the noise gets louder and then the door bursts open and Marley Hayes strides in with a posse of kids at his heels.

'Made it!' he says, shaking the tousled fringe out of his eyes. 'Not too late for the auditions, are we?'

'Auditions?' I echo.

And then I blink and swallow hard, because there has clearly been some kind of mistake. A mistake of epic proportions.

Marley is carrying an electric guitar. Two of the kids behind him are manhandling a full-sized drum kit, complete with cymbals and hi-hat, and behind that I'm sure I can see kids with a cello, a trumpet, a flute . . . and more. Much more.

The kids swarm into the meeting room, filling the space. The beautiful, popular girl with the sad eyes is there, carrying a ukelele. A tall, stringy boy in old-fashioned tortoiseshell glasses slides a bow across his cello. Marley's brother, Dylan, sets up the drum kit and runs through an impressive and ear-splitting drum solo while half a dozen kids I have never seen before in my life sit down and start unpacking instruments and musical scores.

'What are you doing?' I ask Marley. 'Who are all these people?'

Marley grins. 'You know – the poster!' he says. 'I promised to spread the word, and I did! I told everyone I could think of with musical talent. I mean, I know you probably can't take us all, but . . . well, we're keen! Maybe you could give us a chance!'

I blink, baffled.

'A chance at what?' I ask.

48

Marley rolls his eyes. 'Well, the auditions, of course!' he declares. 'For the group. Like it said on the poster! What's the name of it again? Oh yeah – the Lost & Found! Catchy!'

On the other side of the room, I see Bex hiding her head in her hands. From the way her shoulders are shaking, I can't be sure if she's laughing or crying, but I think it's probably the former.

'Um . . . I think there's some mistake,' I tell Marley. 'The Lost & Found . . . it's not that kind of group.'

He raises an eyebrow. 'What kind of group is it then?' he wants to know. 'More . . . folky? Yeah, I should have thought, you with your tambourine and all that. Well, we can adapt . . .'

I shake my head, and Marley's eyes skim over Happi and Romy, both known for their violin skills. 'Classical, maybe?' he guesses, his eyes scanning onwards towards Bex. 'Or . . . Death Metal? Thrash punk?'

I sigh. 'It's not a musical group at all, OK?' I explain. 'Not a band. Just a group. Of people. Meeting up every now and then.'

Marley stops in his tracks. 'Not a band?' he echoes. 'But . . . the poster said . . . I was so sure . . .'

49

'I told you I wasn't musical,' I remind him. 'I meant it!'

'I thought you were joking,' he says, wide-eyed.

Dylan pulls the welcome poster off the meeting-room door and waves it at me. 'This is painted on music paper,' he argues. 'It must be a band!'

Bex steps up beside me. 'The one at school was painted on a map,' she points out. 'So what? This is not a hill-walking group, either. Aren't you listening?'

Dylan frowns, and the rest of them seem equally crestfallen.

'I don't get it . . . what *is* this group for?' Marley demands. 'What does it do?'

I bite my lip. 'It's just . . . a group for anyone feeling a bit lost or out of their depth to meet up with other like-minded kids. That's all.'

'You just sit around . . . talking and eating cake?' he checks.

'What's wrong with that?'

Marley looks sceptical. 'So let's get this straight . . . before we turned up, you had, what, you and four other people? Not much of a group is it?'

'It's a start,' I argue.

'Actually, I was just leaving,' the sandy-haired boy mutters. 'I have an urgent appointment. At the . . . um . . . dentist . . .'

'I'd better be going too,' Romy says, wiping cake crumbs from her lips. 'Sorry, Happi, but a group where people sit around talking about gloomy stuff – well, it's not for me. Anyhow, I told my mum I wouldn't be long.'

Marley shakes his head. 'You're going to let her leave?' he asks me. 'This girl is seriously talented at the violin, and so is your mate Happi. I've heard them play. And you said yourself you play tambourine! Come on, Lexie. Face it. Your idea may have flopped, but fate sent you us instead. We all love music. We're here to audition. Let us play!'

A cheer goes up from the newcomers, and the boy with the trumpet blows an ear-splitting fanfare. I spot Miss Walker's anxious face peering through the glass panel of the door, her candy-pink beehive bobbing up and down. I refuse to catch her eye.

'It's not that kind of group,' I repeat, hopeless now. 'I'm sorry, but the Lost & Found is not a band. I don't know anything at all about being in a band, or holding auditions. Sorry.'

Their smiles slide away into dismay.

'Shame,' Bex comments casually. 'Marley's right about one thing – would have been a cool name for a band.'

All eyes are on me suddenly, and the weight of their disappointment and disapproval is crushing. My patience, stretched to breaking point, finally snaps.

'Oh, do what you like!' I snap. 'I don't care any more! Whatever!'

Marley grins. 'That's settled then. We're a band. Don't worry, Lexie. You don't have to do anything – we'll run these auditions democratically. Everyone can have a go at playing or singing or whatever, and we can all vote for who we think is best! You stay right here, Miss Violin Girl, and you . . . aren't you that new kid in Year Eight? We all know you don't really have a dentist's appointment, so sit down and help Lexie keep a record of who's playing and what they're good at!'

The sandy-haired boy sits down, grinning, and Romy just glows with pride. Everyone seems thrilled at the prospect of a Lost & Found group that involves guitars and tambourines instead of soul searching, which makes me feel a little sad. Although at least this way we still have a group, and it does include some of the kids I've been worrying about. And Marley himself, of course.

He winks at me, grinning, and I can feel my frosty glare begin to thaw a little.

The Lost & Found

Ice-Breakers

* Ask everybody to introduce themselves and say why they are feeling lost or alone.
* Ask everyone to chat to the person next to them and find out three interesting things.
* Ask people what they want from the Lost & Found group.

— Well, a rock band, clearly. 😕

Marley Hayes — lead guitar, electric-acoustic (awesome — knew he would be)

Dylan Hayes — drums (a bit chaotic, but not bad — must be a musical family)

George Clark — cello (tall, pale, stringy with thick glasses — a bit squeaky in places, but with practice could sound OK)

Sasha Kaminski — vocals and ukelele (hopeless on the uke, but would be a fab lead singer — very soulful, bluesy voice)

Lee Mackintosh — trumpet (a bit eccentric and unpredictable . . . but that trumpet! Wow!)

<u>Soumia Murad</u> — keyboards (very cool girl — wears a hijab with a mini skirt and jeggings; quite basic keyboard skills, but serious and determined)

<u>Sami Tagara</u> — flute (never seen this kid before ... sort of silent and sulky, but boy can he play the flute!)

Also ...

<u>Romy Thomas</u> — violin (no violins here so no audition, but like Happi she's been playing for years)

<u>Happi Akebi</u> — violin (as above re violin, but she's brilliant, brilliant, brilliant, obvs)

<u>Bex Murray</u> — bass guitar (no bass guitar here, but she's in Marley's group for guitar lessons and he says she's prob the best he's ever heard — she scowled and rolled her eyes, but I could tell she was pleased)

<u>Jake Cooke</u> — I asked if he could play anything and he said no, but he offered to be the roadie and tech guy ... or learn the triangle

<u>Me</u> — tambourine (I'm probably the worst of the lot — and whoever heard of someone in a band who just played tambourine?)

7

The Lost & Found

Sami Tagara is just finishing a flute solo that makes my eyes prickle with tears when there is a polite knock on the meeting-room door and Miss Walker's face peers in, nervous but smiling.

I jump to my feet. 'Miss Walker!' I exclaim. 'I'm really sorry about the noise! We had a last-minute change of plan. The group has had a bit of a musical theme today. I hope we didn't disturb you!'

'It's been very entertaining!' she says, beaming. 'Several of the regulars have commented. I'm more of a Buddy Holly fan myself, but I'm always open to new influences. I especially liked the cello piece!'

George Clark blushes a beetroot colour and tries to hide behind a curtain of mousy hair, while I thank my lucky stars that Miss Walker is an especially cool and open-minded kind of librarian.

'I just wanted to let you know it's almost seven,' she says, and I blink because somehow two whole hours have flashed by without me even noticing. 'I'll need to lock up soon . . .'

Time has hurtled past in a blur of music, chat and chocolate traybakes. My misfits support group may be a non-starter, but its rapid evolution into a fledgling band has been nothing short of awesome.

'Oh . . . sorry,' I apologize again. 'We were only supposed to be here till six, weren't we? We got a bit carried away . . .'

'Not a problem,' the librarian insists. 'We can easily change it to a two-hour slot. Will you be needing the room again next week?'

'Er . . .'

'Definitely,' Marley cuts in. 'Every Monday for the foreseeable future. Although two nights a week would be even better!'

I frown. 'Unless the noise is going to be a problem?'

57

'Not a bit,' Miss Walker grins. 'Libraries aren't the silent, dusty places people imagine, you know. We have the Over-65s Bingo Club in here on a Tuesday afternoon, and they're far rowdier than you lot! Now let me see . . . There's a two-hour slot free on a Thursday evening; shall I pencil you in for that?'

'Yes please!' I say, and the door clicks shut again.

'So,' Marley says. 'We have a lot of talent in this room . . . but do we have a band? How do we whittle things down to a manageable size? Free vote? Or a secret ballot – would that be better?'

I sigh. 'I guess. It's a shame we have to whittle it down, though. Like you say, there's a lot of talent here.'

'We didn't even get to hear you play,' Marley frowns. 'Nor Happi, nor Romy. So the vote might not be all that fair . . . Happi and Romy are proper musos. Plus, the group was your idea, so you kind of have to be in it . . .'

Bex turns from stacking chairs. 'Who says a band has to have four or five members anyway? Why not eight or nine or ten?'

'Not practical,' Marley argues. 'Be a nightmare to organize. Bands just aren't that big!'

58

'Some are,' Bex protests. 'What about Arcade Fire? Or Gogol Bordello? Or So Solid Crew? When it works, it can be amazing.'

'We'd be mad to turn people away,' Dylan chips in. 'We've got the most musically gifted kids in the school in this room right now. Why not work with it? See where it takes us?'

Marley shrugs. 'Well, it's your band,' he says, his blue eyes holding mine. 'What do you think, Lexie? Vote, or keep everyone?'

It's a no-brainer, of course. The whole idea of the Lost & Found group was to bring people together, include anyone who wanted to be included. Maybe . . . just maybe . . . a band can do that even better than a support group. I glance down at my notebook. One thing's for sure: no ice-breakers will be necessary.

'Everybody's in,' I decide. 'Like Marley said . . . maybe there were a few crossed wires over the poster, but it really is like fate has played a trick and thrown us together. The Lost & Found may be the most . . . unexpected group ever, but it's going to be the best. I know it!'

A roar of approval erupts, finished off nicely by a

euphoric trumpet blast, and Bex raises her paper cup of orange squash high in the air.

'To the Lost & Found,' she says. 'The biggest and best and most awesomely brilliant band to come out of Millford. Well, the only band, actually. But still. To us!'

'All eleven of us,' Marley chimes in.

'Twelve,' I say, winking at Jake Cooke. 'To us!'

Dear Mum,

Remember when I was little, in Scotland, and you showed me how to make a musical shaker by putting dried lentils in an old margarine tub and painting the outside with acrylic paint? Remember how I loved it?

I never was all that musical, but things have got kind of muddled up here and I seem to be in a band with Happi and Bex and a load of other people I don't even know. I'm supposed to be playing the tambourine, so I can't go too far wrong, hopefully. It's all a bit weird, but it might be fun.

I'll keep you posted!

Love,
Lexie x

8

I'm With the Band

Overnight, our friendship group widens. Instead of sitting in our usual huddle of three at lunchtime, we are joined by Jake Cooke, Sasha Kaminski and Romy Thomas. It's a little awkward, but everyone smiles a lot and at least we have something to talk about. The rest of the canteen seem kind of curious too, judging by the looks and whispers we're getting.

Jake says he's willing to help with anything – ideas, sound, tech stuff, whatever. 'I just want to be useful!' he says.

Sasha wants to know what type of music we'll be playing, and whether I've thought about band identity and styling. I tell her I haven't, and scribble a note in my jotter to think about those things. It's all a little bit overwhelming.

Romy just wants somewhere to sit that isn't in the corner all alone, and I feel guilty that I hadn't thought of inviting her to hang out with us before. She looks so obviously lost.

A hard-faced girl with a mouth full of chewing gum stops at our table. 'Are you Lexie?' she asks me. 'You're with the band, right? Marley said I should speak to you.'

I straighten my shoulders. 'Yes, I'm Lexie. I'm with the band.'

I like the sound of that. I like it a lot.

'So . . . can I help you?'

'Depends,' the girl says. 'See, I'm, like, a really, really good singer. I can do Adele, I can do Rihanna . . . whoever you want. Everyone says I should go on the *X Factor*. I mentioned it to Marley in French this morning and he told me to let you know . . .'

'We've got a singer already,' Bex replies. 'Sasha here. But if we need anyone else at any point, we'll definitely keep you in mind!'

The hard-faced girl curls her lip.

63

'I might not be available by then,' she says. 'I have a lot of offers on the table just now. And once I audition for the *X Factor*, that's that, obviously – I'll be under contract. I was just thinking you might like the help, y'know . . . a voice that'll get you noticed. Marley's a friend of mine, so it was kind of a favour for him. He'll be upset you can't fit me in, but hey. No skin off my nose.'

She casts a disgusted look round the table, and I panic and wonder if Bex has been too hasty. If Marley sent her, he must think she's good, surely? I am tempted to say she can join if she wants to, but Bex is too quick for me.

'We can't,' she says sweetly. 'Sorry, Sharleen. You should have auditioned yesterday, like everyone else. I'm surprised Marley didn't mention it to you before . . . what with you being practically a superstar and all.'

Sharleen rolls her eyes.

'Your loss,' she snarls. 'A word of advice, though. You should be a little bit more picky about who you have in your band. I mean . . . geeky little weirdos and talentless airheads and fat, ugly losers aren't exactly going to pull in the crowds, are they? I need a professional backing band, not a freak show. Whatever!'

She stalks away, leaving us all a little shell-shocked.

'Who was that?' Jake asks, wide-eyed. 'What just happened, even?'

'Sharleen Scott, well-known Year Ten bully,' Bex explains. 'Vain and spiteful with a cruel streak thrown in for good measure.'

'I know her well,' Sasha says sadly.

'Me too,' Romy whispers.

OK. Narrow escape, clearly. Although bullies may be just as lost as the rest of us – more so, probably. Guilt washes over me.

'Were we . . . maybe . . . just a little bit harsh?' I wonder out loud.

'Us?' Bex snorts. 'Wise up, Lexie. That girl is bad news. Come to think of it, Marley is bad news too. And me, possibly. Trust me, there is only so much of that you can have in a band.'

'I think she used to go out with Marley,' Happi comments.

'So did half the girls in this school,' Bex says. 'I don't care who she used to date, we don't want her messing up this project. Seriously, Lexie.'

I bite my lip.

'She just called us all geeky little weirdos, Lexie,' Happi reminds me.

'She called me a talentless airhead,' Sasha adds. 'Nice.'

'And, well, you heard what she called me,' Romy whispers. 'She's right, isn't she? I don't fit in. I am overweight, and I am . . . well, the rest. It's not the first time I've been called fat and ugly, and it won't be the last. I don't belong in the band. I should have known it was too good to be true . . .'

Her eyes brim with tears, and I know that if I don't say something fast this whole band will crumble into dust before it even gets started.

'Romy, stop right there. You're going nowhere,' I declare. 'You're an amazing musician – we're lucky to have you. The Lost & Found is not about looks or weight, not that I'm saying you have anything to worry about in either area, obviously . . .'

I stumble to a halt before I get into any more of a tangle. The truth is that Romy is overweight; her hair is lank and her skin is sprinkled with blackheads. She looks pale and tired, as if she doesn't get enough sleep and doesn't see enough sunshine.

 66

'Do I look like I'm in a band?' Happi challenges. 'Do any of us? C'mon, Romy. We're just a big bunch of musical misfits, that's all. Nobody cares – only Sharleen, and she's full of poison and spite. Why waste time listening to her nastiness?'

Romy tries for a shaky smile.

'We're a work in progress, anyhow,' Sasha states. 'We don't look like a band yet – but we will! None of us are perfect, but we can help each other! Maybe we could come up with a logo for a T-shirt design, or just go for a certain image – rock or punk or pop or vintage, whatever. The main thing is to ignore bullies like Sharleen. Seriously, Romy. I plan to.'

'Me too,' Happi agrees. 'Who needs that stuff?'

'As for her singing skills,' Bex cuts in, 'She has a voice like fingernails scraping across a chalkboard, with overtones of cats being strangled.'

Jake laughs. 'We haven't even existed for a day yet, and already we're causing a stir,' he says. 'People want to know what we're up to; people want to join. We should definitely be running a publicity campaign, do some posters, cash in on the speculation – keep people guessing!'

'Social media too,' Happi says. 'Facebook, Twitter, Instagram, all the usual suspects . . .'

I write all this down in my notebook. I can see that the Lost & Found may turn out to be quite a bit of work, but I don't care – it's exciting. It feels like we're on the edge of something cool, something awesome. Maybe.

We go back to our dinners; Bex and Jake are bonding over marketing ideas, Happi, Sasha and Romy forming an unlikely alliance to discuss style and image. I can hear Sasha whispering to Romy about a really good shampoo for shiny hair as I dig into my chocolate pudding and custard.

Suddenly Bex jabs me in the ribs. 'Bob Brother alert,' she hisses. 'Incoming!'

'Who are the Bob Brothers?' Jake asks, but Bex kicks him under the table and he falls into silence.

Out of nowhere, Marley saunters over, grinning, guitar slung over his shoulder.

'Hey,' he says. 'How's my favourite girl?'

I feel my cheeks turning a pale shade of crimson. 'Don't know . . . How is she?' I quip. 'Who is she? Tell all!'

'She's you, idiot,' Marley says, sliding into the chair next to me. 'Stop playing hard to get! You're my musical genius

68

partner-in-crime, and you know it. We need to have a band meeting, put some plans and ideas on the table. What d'you think? Just an informal thing – get stuff sorted before our first official practice?'

'Cool,' I reply, because this is Marley Hayes asking, after all. I push my plate away and wipe a crumb of chocolate pudding from the corner of my mouth.

'I've just met a friend of yours,' I say. 'Sharleen Scott. She said you recommended her for the band . . .'

Marley slaps a hand over his face. 'No way,' he wails. 'She has a voice like a bag of rusty nails and a personality to match. Please say you told her no?'

I laugh. 'Bex did . . . thank goodness!'

'Phew,' Marley says. 'That could have been tricky. So . . . band meeting? Somewhere a bit . . . quieter? After school?'

I grin. 'I guess so. I'll put the word out, and you can too, and hopefully most people will be able to make it . . .'

Marley grins. 'No – just you, Lexie, if that's OK? What with the band being your idea and stuff. Or yours and mine, maybe. We can get together as a group on Thursday, as planned, but you and I need to get stuff mapped out before that . . .'

I blink.

Marley Hayes wants to talk to me – just me – about the band? Somewhere quieter? My cheeks flare. I am turning red more often than a traffic light since meeting this boy.

'Sure,' I mutter, attempting nonchalance. 'No worries . . .'

'I'll wait for you by the main gate after school,' Marley says. 'See you then!'

He's gone, leaving me speechless and slightly stunned. I look up at the others and find them all staring at me, clearly amused.

'So . . . what's this Bob Brother thing?' Jake repeats, taking the heat off me for a moment. 'Is it to do with his name being Marley? After Bob Marley?'

'Spot on,' Bex says. 'And his brother's called Dylan, after Bob Dylan I'm guessing, so . . . they're the Bob Brothers. Make sense?'

'Got it,' Jake says. 'Cool.'

Bex turns her attention to me. 'They're both trouble, obviously,' she says. 'But Marley's the worst. He's had more girlfriends than we've had hot dinners, and now it looks like he's got his eye on Lexie . . .'

'Yeah, Lexie,' Happi comments, raising an eyebrow. 'I think the school bad boy just asked you on a date.'

'Look,' I say. 'His reputation is wildly exaggerated. I mean sure, he's a little bit lost and maybe he has a knack for trouble . . . but none of us are perfect, right? He's OK. Really. And besides, it's just business.'

'Keep telling yourself that, Lexie,' Bex says, laughing. 'But I'm telling you . . . that boy does not have business on his mind!'

My eyes follow Marley as he swipes a chip from the plate of an outraged Year Seven kid, then pushes through the double doors and out into the corridor without a backward glance.

LOST & FOUND

- What kind of sound do we want?
  Punk, rock, rap, pop, indie, reggae,
  folk, jazz, funk, soul, R&B?

- Make a list of songs to learn/ play

- What kind of look do we want?

- Discuss logo

- Do we need a manager? Jake?

- Social media?

- Aim towards a gig at some point?
  School summer fete?
  School open evening?

9

The Leaping Llama

The Leaping Llama Cafe is one of those painfully hipster places where the barista has a beard the size of a small koala bear and skinny jeans with turn-ups that end three inches above his bare ankles. I think they probably vet people at the door to make sure they're cool enough to enter, and because I am with Marley I have somehow been allowed to slip through the net.

It must be that, unless my outsize black school sweater, grey woolly tights and red bobble hat are hipster enough to pass the test.

We sit in a corner booth sipping hot chocolate, Marley's guitar propped up on the seat beside him. His blue eyes blaze with enthusiasm as he talks about the band, and I'm transfixed.

'We have to get this sorted before Thursday,' he's saying. 'The others will be looking to us for direction. There's such a buzz going round the school about all this . . . Let's see if we can keep it going! Any thoughts?'

I push my notebook across the table towards him, and he frowns.

'What kind of sound?' he reads aloud. 'Well, indie I think . . . with overtones of folk and jazz because of the violins, the cello and the trumpet. We'll find our own sound, don't worry. And as for shortlisting songs to learn . . . we don't want to go down that track, surely? Playing covers of other people's songs?'

I put my mug of hot chocolate down.

'So . . . we have original songs? Already?'

'Well, kind of . . .'

Marley unzips his guitar case and starts to strum, without any awkwardness at all. His fingers pick expertly at the strings, and a sweet kaleidoscope of sound curls around us, dredging unnamed feelings to the surface, telling a story of unexpected sadness and joy. The koala-beard barista

74

stops serving to lean on the counter and listen, and the people in the coffee queue turn to face us as the music reaches a crescendo and dies away at last. The staff and customers of the Leaping Llama give Marley a round of applause, with a few whistles and whoops thrown in for good measure.

'Awesome,' I say. 'I mean, just . . . wow! Did you write that?'

Marley shrugs. 'Sounds better with an amp and some backing, but, yeah, music I don't have a problem with,' he explains. 'It's the words I can't do. I know what I want to say, I just . . . it's not my skill, finding the words to express it all. And obviously a song needs both elements. So I was wondering . . . you're good with words, right?'

I blink. 'Me? Words?'

Marley frowns. 'I've seen you around,' he says. 'Waiting outside the hall after school for Happi to finish orchestra practice . . . reading. In the park in the summer with Bex, in the sunshine . . . reading. On the bus to town . . . reading. Always reading. So you must be good with words. Stands to reason.'

75

'Well, reading them is not the same as writing them,' I point out.

'You're good at writing them too, though,' he tells me. 'I remember. I was in Year Six when you joined my primary school . . . you were in Year Five, in Dylan's class, remember? It was almost the end of the school year, and the whole of the junior school put on a special assembly for the Year Six leavers. Year Five had rehearsed a play, Year Four had learned some songs . . . but you turned up too late in the term to do any of that.'

I nod, remembering . . .

'We could get you to read out a poem, instead,' the teacher had said. 'Would you like that, Lexie?'

So I had gone away and written a poem about leaving, moving on, and how it was happy and sad at the same time. When I'd showed it to the teacher next day she'd told me it was perfect and asked me where I'd found it, and when I told her I'd written it myself she got all misty-eyed for a minute. It turned out she'd meant me to read a poem out of a book, but she said that this one was much better.

I'd stood on stage and tried not to be scared and read my poem, and it seems that Marley had been listening.

'I loved that poem,' he says now. 'And when the teacher told us you'd written it I was dead envious. Like I said, words aren't my thing, but they are yours. I've had my eye on you for a while, Lexie Lawlor!'

I'm kind of speechless. Marley Hayes knows who I am . . . knew who I was all this time. The information clatters through my brain like the ticker-tape updates of breaking news you get on TV when something cataclysmic has happened. I'm incapable of thinking of anything else.

Gorgeous Boy With Cute Fringe And Dangerous Eyes Notices Quiet Book Geek And Accidentally Invents Band With Her . . . I feel dizzy at the very idea.

'You're staring,' Marley says with a grin. 'Don't get me wrong – I quite like being stared at, but it's a little bit unnerving. Have I got cake crumbs in my fringe or something?'

'No!' I say. 'No cake crumbs. Sorry!'

I gaze at the tabletop instead, wondering why I have suddenly lost the ability to act like a normal human being.

'So . . . will you have a go?' Marley is saying. 'At writing some lyrics for the song? What with you being brilliant with words, like I said.'

77

'I'm not, though!' I argue. 'I can't write lyrics. I've never done anything like that before! A song's not just about words, is it? Or even music. There's more to it than that!'

Marley nods, and his blue eyes laugh as they hook on to mine.

'Obviously,' he agrees. 'That's why I'm asking you — you're clever, you're sensitive, you get all that. A song is much more than words and music. A song is like all these mad, raw feelings, squashed into just three or four minutes of music. It's . . . I dunno, love and death and hate and fear and joy and glory and shame . . . everything! It makes you think, makes you understand stuff. A good song worms its way inside your soul and becomes, like, a part of you!'

'I thought you were rubbish with words?' I say.

'I've tried, Lexie,' he tells me. 'I know what I want to say, but I just can't do it. I express myself best in music, not words. But you . . . you could have a try, maybe? Just have a go? We need lyrics by Thursday . . .'

'Thursday? But . . . today's Tuesday! That's less than forty-eight hours to turn a piece of music into a song . . .

78

from scratch! Have you got the sheet music for this? Anything written down?'

Marley frowns. 'I'm not big on writing down the chords,' he says. 'I just sort of hear it in my head, and make it happen, and record it on GarageBand. Keep it simple, right?'

But this is a million miles from simple. I am way, way out of my depth.

'I can't, Marley!' I argue. 'I've never written a song before. I just . . . wouldn't know where to start!'

He rakes a hand through his hair. 'Start where I always do,' he suggests. 'Hook on to a feeling . . . something big . . . and let it swamp you. Let it wash right over you, soak you through . . . and ride the wave. That's what I do!'

I am gazing at Marley as if I have lost my mind, and maybe I actually have. My eyes are glazed and my mouth is slightly open, and I know I must look stunned and adoring and possibly slightly unhinged, but Marley is probably used to that. I mean, it's not just that he looks gorgeous, he's clever and creative and crazily talented . . . and he wants to work with me.

Somehow he makes it all seem possible . . . songwriting, the band . . . life.

'D'you know what I mean?' He nudges me, and I snap out of my trance. 'You don't need sheet music or rules or worries about whether you've done it before. Keep it free. Feelings, yeah?'

I blink. 'Uh? Um . . . yeah!' I say, miraculously recovering the power of speech. 'Feelings. Got it.'

'You live with Bex Murray, right?' he says gently. 'And Bex is in foster, so I'm guessing you must be too. I remember you, Lexie, and not just for that poem. You were all sad back then, but you're not like that now. You're smart, sassy, sparky, but there's still something about you . . . something hidden, something deep.'

I want to argue, say that everyone has something sad or difficult to carry – stuff they don't talk about – but I'm silent. I can feel my heart beating hard. All this time, I thought I'd been invisible . . . but Marley could see me. Marley believes in me.

'Give me your email and social media links,' he says, holding out his phone. 'I'll send you a GarageBand link later. It's only rough, obviously – I'm imagining violin and

 80

keyboards and a gentle drumbeat, and vocal harmonies, obviously . . . Can you see it?'

I'm like a rabbit in the headlights. I can't see anything but Marley's blue eyes, blazing with fire and energy, but I am not about to admit that.

'Yes . . . yes, I can see it,' I bluff. 'Awesome.'

Marley grins. 'I think we'll make a great team, Lexie!' he says. 'You're on my wavelength – you understand me. I have a vision for this band, and you can see it too . . . How cool is that?'

'Cool,' I say. 'Seriously cool.'

'I'm relying on you to help me do this,' he says. 'I mean, eleven people . . . It's not going to be easy to pull everyone together and get the best from them all. But I totally love that you can see their potential – that you want to include us all!'

The koala-beard barista is wiping tables and stacking chairs around us, and Marley takes the hint and packs up his guitar.

'You came up with the best ever name for the band,' he says, as we mooch out of the door. 'Lost & Found . . . it's great. Perfect. We've all felt lost at some point, right? Every single teenager in the world can relate. Genius.'

He looks at me, blue eyes hooked on to mine, that fringe falling messily over his face, and I know I'm hopelessly lost, so lost I may never find myself again.

I don't even care.

Dear Mum,

This is a really difficult letter to write. I wish I
could say it out loud to you and not write it
down. I wish you were here to listen.

The thing is, I've met a boy. He's cute, so cute
that half the school is after him, so I have literally
no chance anyway, but it doesn't stop me liking
him. I think he likes me too, but he's a born flirt
so I could be wrong... he might be like that with
everyone. I just can't tell.

I don't think I've ever liked anyone like this
before, and it's all a bit scary. It's not the sort of
thing I can talk to Happi or Bex about, or even
Mandy. I'd just feel so shy and awkward. Mary
Shelley, maybe? I wish you were here. You'd
understand – I know you would.

Love,
Lexie x

10

Left Behind

Strong feelings? I could pick anything from the last three years, but why not be brave and go right back to the day Mum left?

Anger, sadness, shame, fear . . . It was all there. Anger that Mum had been gone too long; sadness that she'd left me behind; shame that I was so scared, so anxious; and fear, a big black shadow I could see from the corner of my eye wherever I looked, whatever I did.

I watched *Frozen* five times that first day. I was afraid to sit alone in the silence, watching the hands on the kitchen clock creep round. I was afraid to believe that Mum had gone.

I invented stories to explain her absence.

Maybe she'd been offered a job and told to start immediately. Maybe she'd been spotted by a model agency or a famous photographer and asked to star in a photo shoot. Maybe she'd bumped into my dad again after all these years and the two of them were catching up on old times. Maybe she was just waiting for the right moment to tell him he had a daughter . . .

Maybe, maybe, maybe.

I switched off the DVD.

It was past midnight by then, and I knew that, no matter how many maybes I could think up, there was no way on earth Mum would leave me alone all that time. I fetched my duvet from the bedroom and made myself a nest on the sofa.

I tried to sleep, but the maybes got darker.

Maybe Mum had been in an accident. Maybe she'd been kidnapped, knocked unconscious, captured by spies. Maybe she was sick, lying in a hospital with broken bones or a fever, unable to remember her name, her home, her life?

I cried a bit, and then, at last, I slept.

The next day, I was sure that Mum would come home, with a smile, a hug, an explanation. I made the most of my freedom, eating Coco Pops for breakfast and rereading my library books. Mum didn't appear. I remembered what she'd said to me about feeling lost. I hadn't taken it seriously at the time. What had she meant?

I thought of all the places I could go to look for her. The job centre, the library, the park, the corner shop, the cafe that did milkshakes with ice-cream floats.

There was a problem, though . . . I was nine years old and I didn't have a key for the flat. Mum always met me from school and walked me home. Would it be safe to go out and leave the door ajar? I was pretty sure it wouldn't. Besides, what if I went out to look for Mum and she came home while I was gone?

When I was very small and the two of us were in a shopping centre or supermarket or any place that was big and busy, we had a rule. If we got separated, I was to stay calm and stay where I was, and Mum would come to find me.

This was different, obviously. Mum was the one who was lost, not me, but still it made sense to me that she'd come

86

back here the moment she could. I ate the rest of my chocolate Easter egg that second day, and an apple because Mum always said they were healthy.

On the third day, I worked my way through the kitchen cupboards. Stale digestives, baked beans, the dregs of a jar of pickled onions. I debated going out to knock on one of the other doors on our floor, but Mum had always told me not to talk to the neighbours. There was a bloke who smoked drugs and played his music too loud, a group of eastern European guys, a wild-eyed woman with Tourette's who yelled and swore a lot. I didn't have the courage to go to any of them.

On the fourth day, I found a packet of powdered mousse that you were supposed to mix with milk . . . but there was no milk, so I mixed it with water and drank it like a sweet, sickly soup. The Easter holidays were over by then, but I'd lost track of time. I was drifting in a fog of loss and pain, and hunger gnawed at my guts, an ache that wouldn't go away. I sat beside the window and gazed out of the flat, looked up at the blue sky and the watery sun and then down at the concrete playground and the path that led through the estate, covered in broken glass that sparkled like glitter.

87

I thought that if I watched for long enough, my mum might come walking along that path, smiling. She didn't.

I remember it all.

I cried a lot.

I remember wishing I had a mobile phone, money for the electric meter, food.

I remember wondering if anyone would ever find me.

In the end, school told social services that I wasn't in class and that my mum wasn't responding to texts and calls.

I remember waking up from a half-sleep to the sound of someone banging on the door, and for a moment, just one split second, I thought it was Mum, that she was back, had lost her key somehow. I stumbled across the flat, dragging the duvet behind me, but when I opened the door it wasn't Mum at all. Two police officers, a man in a suit and a tired-looking woman who said her name was Josie were on the doorstep.

They asked a million questions about Mum, and when I couldn't answer they told me to pack some clothes and grab a toothbrush. I was being taken into care. I held on to Muttley the knitted dog, packed my library books so they

88

wouldn't go overdue and held on to Josie's hand. I walked out of the flat and into a different world.

I'm writing, pencil scratching across the paper so fast I can't keep track of what I'm saying. It doesn't seem to matter about rhymes or patterns or whether the words resemble a song, just that those words are out there. They're scary words: raw, painful, beautiful. I realize I am crying as I write. I can feel the pain inside me, memories leaking out of my eyes, sliding down my cheeks as fat, salty tears.

Mary Shelley blinks at me, concerned, but I can't stop.

I work on, Marley's guitar piece playing on repeat in the background. I cross out phrases, lines, paragraphs, move things around. The story changes, simplifies, slides off on a tangent. It becomes bigger, smaller, stronger. It's still my story, but it feels like everyone's story at the same time.

I keep working until the words fit themselves to the music, lodging themselves in place as if they have always been that way. I am whispering, singing softly to myself as I write, scribbling things down, changing things around. I feel shy at first, worried in case Mandy and Jon hear me and wonder what I'm doing, but after a while the stop-start crooning,

89

the singing to myself, becomes second nature. I record myself on my phone, singing along to Marley's backing piece, then alter two of the verses and tweak the chorus and record it all again with some tambourine backing.

It's messy, emotional, rough around the edges, but I love it.

I keep on working until I have a song.

Back Then

I used to be a nomad child,
They said I was a little wild.
Nothing I wouldn't dare to do
Because I was with you.
I used to be so many things
Back then.

Chorus: The stars are flung across a velvet sky
         Like broken glass, like broken dreams.
         I think the stars can hear me cry,
         Or that's the way it seems.

I used to be so many things,
Used to want to spread my wings.
I thought the world was all for me –
Nothing that I couldn't be,
Nothing that I couldn't do,
Back then.

Chorus

Nothing that I couldn't do
But nothing I believed was true.
Please tell me why you went away,
Why you thought that I should stay.

Why it had to end that way,
Back then.

<u>Chorus</u>

I can't remember how it was.
I can't remember it because
I darent look back.
I'll stay on track,
Won't think about the life I had
Back then.

<u>Chorus</u>

11

Band Practice

I'm miles away, in a different time, a different place. I'm watching the big library bus draw up in the village square, back when we lived in the cottage in Scotland. I remember running up the steps, racing to the end of the bus where the children's books were.

'Oh, this one was my favourite too when I was your age,' Mum had said as she sat down beside me on a beanbag. '*The Tiger Who Came to Tea* . . .'

She scooped me up on to her lap and I snuggled close. I could smell her sweet vanilla scent, feel the warmth of her breath on the back of my neck as she read out the story . . .

*

93

'You OK, Lexie?' Bex asks, and I snap back to the present.

'Yeah . . . sure!'

As we head into the library, a motley crew of mismatched kids lugging a drum kit, keyboards and assorted other instruments, Miss Walker seems distant, distracted and anxious. Her poodle-print circle skirt and scarlet twinset seem out of place today and, though she raises a half-hearted smile and brings us a tray of hot chocolate and cookies, I can see that something is very wrong.

'What's up, Miss W?' Bex asks, direct as always. 'Has something happened?'

Miss Walker puts a finger to her lips and gestures across the library to where two men in suits are noting things down on clipboards.

'A visit from the council,' she whispers. 'An audit, whatever that is. No warning. I'm sure it's nothing to worry about, but on top of all the talk of cuts and the public consultations . . . well, those two have got me spooked. Won't have a cup of tea, won't chat with the library users, don't want to see the figures . . .'

The men in suits look sulky and sour, but I'm sure Miss Walker is worrying over nothing.

'They can't do anything,' I say. 'Can they? People love this library!'

'Of course they do,' Bex agrees. 'Someone even got up a petition when they started up with all that rubbish about cutting hours. Don't worry – it'll be OK!'

But Miss Walker doesn't seem convinced, and I can tell that Bex is remembering the way Millford Park Academy closed its library over the summer holidays last year, quietly and without discussion. It doesn't always matter how many people care about something. Sometimes, it just comes down to numbers on a spreadsheet, balancing books, making savings.

'We have the highest footfall of any of the local libraries in Millford; the highest book traffic,' Miss Walker is saying. 'That should be in our favour, but these guys won't talk about that – won't talk about anything. They've been taking photographs of the damp patch on the wall over by the computers and photographs of the window frames – they do need replacing, I suppose, but we manage! This library was built in the 1920s, and it hasn't fallen down yet . . .'

'Maybe they're planning a renovation?' I suggest. 'New windows and a damp-proof course?'

95

'In our dreams,' Miss Walker says.

'Bex is right – it'll be OK,' I insist, looking around the place. 'I mean . . . just look!'

Parents and toddlers are sitting on brightly coloured cushions, reading picture books; schoolkids are browsing the children's section; adults of all ages and varieties are wandering along the shelves of fiction and non-fiction, and every computer in the place is being used. On a central table, the Thursday Knit & Natter group is in full swing – five elderly ladies drinking tea and knitting rainbow squares to make a quilt for Syrian refugees. And then there's us, the noisy teenagers, setting up for band practice in the community meeting room.

It's pretty much the perfect library, but Miss Walker still looks worried.

'Are we still all right to practise?' Bex checks. 'The noise won't be a problem, will it? With those blokes here?'

Miss Walker sighs and dredges up a smile. 'Oh, Bex, Lexie, you kids go ahead,' she says. 'That's what the community meeting room is for. I don't know what that pair are up to, but they're not going to stop us from

96

doing what we're supposed to do. Take no notice of me, pet!'

'We won't be too noisy,' I say, although I think perhaps we will. 'We only have one busking amp between us. We'll try to keep it down . . .'

That promise gets broken straight away.

It's absolute, total chaos.

Eleven musicians and one tech guy squashed into a small room with a drum kit, a keyboard, two guitars, a flute, a trumpet, a cello and assorted other instruments, along with a mic and a busking amp . . . It was never going to be easy. At least on Monday people took it in turns – this time we're attempting to play together, and it's a nightmare. People are tuning up, chatting, breaking into little groups of two or three to play favourite songs.

At one point, we have Nirvana's 'Smells Like Teen Spirit' going up against 'Good Riddance' by Green Day and 'Jolene' by Dolly Parton. It's all kind of traumatic, and I peer through the window of the meeting-room door in case Miss Walker has changed her mind about the noise, but all I can see is her candy-pink beehive nodding slightly in the distance as she talks to the two guys in suits.

I turn back to the band.

Marley is exasperated too. Unlike me, he is a natural leader, waving his arms and yelling above the cacophony.

'You're a shambles,' he roars, as the racket crashes to a halt. 'Focus! I need you to listen – and think. Listen to this and get the shape of it in your head . . . get the story, the feel of it. Think about where your instrument could add to it. OK?'

Everybody nods.

He starts to play guitar and Sasha, pink-faced, begins to sing the words I've written. I know Marley sent her the rough-cut recording I made of the song, and I cringe thinking of Sasha listening to my imperfect voice mapping out the song. It still feels so personal to me – and now she's singing out for everyone in the band to hear. I can hear that she's been practising, though, stepping inside the lyrics and giving them a clear, sweet clarity.

I feel like someone has peeled my skin back and exposed my insides in all their painful, messy, shameful glory.

 98

Whatever made me think I could drag my feelings up and share them with the world?

Sasha's voice swoops and soars, playing games with my heart; Marley's haunting guitar riffs and his brother's steady drum backing underpin it all. When the sound dies away and I dare to look up I notice Happi has tears in her eyes and Romy has a hand over her mouth and Jake is looking at me as though he has never quite seen me before. The others look transfixed too, silent and respectful.

'Awesome, man,' says Lee, the trumpet boy.

'Beautiful,' Soumia agrees. 'Just tell us what you want us to do!'

Marley does. He instructs Lee to work up a short, soulful trumpet intro, asks Soumia to create a light, piercing keyboard piece to open each verse and tasks Bex with helping to build up a richer sound with her bass guitar. Happi, Romy and George are charged with ramping up the emotion on each chorus, and Sami has the job of linking the verses and chorus with some flutey stuff.

'You can chuck in some tambourine,' Marley says to me. 'Like on the rough cut, OK? And once we've got all that

99

in place, I want you and Romy to try some harmonies – you both have decent voices. Right. One more time!'

We run through the song again, trying to add all that in, but it's too much to keep on top of and we descend into chaos once more. I'm panicking because the whole thing sounds grim, but Marley just takes it in his stride and decides to break things down a bit. He gets Lee working on the intro and Happi, Romy and George on their section, while Soumia runs through her keyboard piece over and over and Sami sits on the edge of it all, face still and guarded, playing something so beautiful on the flute that I get shivers. Romy and I work out some basic backing harmonies, then Romy switches back to violin, working up her part with Happi and George. Lee's trumpet intro is sounding almost perfect.

Slowly it comes together. Marley gets Dylan and Bex to play the song through with him and Sasha, then they run through it again with Lee's trumpet intro and my tambourine. It takes a few tries to get the timing right, but we're all grinning at how good it sounds. Next, Soumia adds her keyboard piece at the start of each verse, and we go over that so many times I think I may lose the will to live, but slowly it falls into place and begins to sound like something cool.

'Backing vocals,' Marley yells, and Romy and I step up to the mic and add our harmonies – and it actually works. Sami comes in with the flute, and finally Marley adds Happi and Romy on violin and George on cello. We plough through it all so many times I start to hate this stupid song, but after a while the whole thing comes together once more, and it sounds glorious.

In a slightly rough-around-the-edges way.

As the last chords fade away, Marley rakes a hand through his fringe, grinning. Sasha looks exhausted but jubilant, and the rest of us are just plain knackered and slightly disbelieving, hardly daring to accept that we've gone from chaos to discipline and wonder in just two hours.

'I think we have a band,' Marley says. 'And I think we have a sound! You're amazing, all of you!'

The practice breaks up, and we pack up and haul away our stuff, and as usual Happi, Bex and I are last, fussing over the chairs, tidying away a stray crisp packet, rinsing the hot chocolate mugs at the sink in Miss Walker's office. It's past seven and the main library lights are off; I can just see Miss Walker quietly stacking shelves in the half-light over by the children's section.

'We're off now . . . Thanks, Miss W!' Bex shouts, and the librarian raises a hand to wave faintly.

'Thank you!' I call, but as Miss Walker turns towards me I see that her cheeks are wet with tears, and the warm spring evening feels suddenly cold.

Dear Men in Suits,

Sorry but I don't know your names,
and I suppose there might be quite a
few men in suits at the town council,
and women in suits as well,
obviously. This letter is to the two
men who came to Bridge Street
Library on Thursday. I don't know
what you said or what you did, but it
made the librarian cry, and I think
that's horrible because she is the
kindest and the most hard-working
librarian I have ever met. With the
coolest hair.

Anyway, I was one of the kids
doing band practice in the library
last night and we did get a bit carried
away and made a bit of a noise.
If that was the problem, then you
should blame us and not Miss Walker.

We are very sorry.

   If I've got this all wrong and you are just planning to fix the damp patch and put in new window frames, apologies. Those things would be very nice, thank you. Anyway, please tell Miss Walker (the librarian) that she's brilliant and make her smile, or give her a pay rise or something, because she deserves it.

Love,
Lexie x

12

Books and Dreams

Last night we'd tried to talk to Miss Walker, but she shooed us away, said not to worry, locked the door and turned away in the darkness.

'I've written a letter,' I tell Bex as we walk to school the next day. 'To the council. I'm just as worried as you are, honest.'

'I'm not worried; I'm furious,' Bex snaps. 'Where did those creeps get off, making Miss Walker cry? We have to find out what's happened, Lexie!'

Bex turns into a side street, a detour that leads to Bridge Street Library, and although I know the place doesn't open until nine, I don't hesitate; I follow. The two of us wait for a while outside the library, sitting on the big sandstone steps.

Mum always took me to the library wherever we were living; she'd use the computers while I looked at the books, and I always borrowed as many as my ticket would allow. Those books had been pure magic to me, stepping stones to a world where anything was possible.

'They're not just books; they're dreams,' Mum told me once, and I knew exactly what she meant.

Mum's been gone a long time now, but I still love that feeling of being in a library, surrounded by books and dreams. Sometimes I imagine I might look up from the shelves and see her sitting at one of the computers, the way she used to . . . In my dreams, she'd be searching the internet for me, trying to track me down, and I'd be right there. There'd be some kind of hazy, slow-mo reunion, all tears and hugs and happy-ever-after, and we'd ride off into the sunset together.

Yeah, right.

That's why I love libraries, though . . . it's not just the books; it's crazy hopes and dreams. Miss Walker didn't bat an eyelid when Bex and I scoured the shelves for books on

106

how to be a detective, or when we read our way through endless Sherlock Holmes and Miss Marple novels. She let me borrow *Frankenstein* because she could see I'd fallen in love with the idea of it. Miss Walker must have scanned and stamped hundreds of books for me: everything from tortoise care and missing persons to Harry Potter. She makes us hot chocolate and lets us make a racket, and I hate the idea of horrible Men in Suits making her cry.

'We'll be late for school, obviously,' Bex says. 'Dental check-up, d'you reckon?'

'Sure,' I agree. 'A little white lie for a good cause doesn't really count . . .'

Miss Walker arrives, keys in hand, pink hair like candyfloss in the spring sunshine. Her face breaks into its usual smile as she sees us, and I tell myself that everything is fine, that we maybe got things wrong last night.

'Hello, Bex! Hello, Lexie!' she says, unlocking the door. 'What's up? Did you leave something last night?'

'Nah . . . we were just worried,' Bex says. 'We wanted to find out what was happening!'

'Yesterday, when we were leaving – you were crying,' I add. 'Is everything OK?'

Miss Walker's smile slides away. 'Oh, girls,' she says. 'It's not OK, not really. We've been kidding ourselves, imagining we could escape the council cuts. The government have slashed funding again and there isn't enough cash to keep all the services running. They're looking for ways to cut back, and they've decided to close all the local libraries and just keep the big one in town.'

Bex says something unprintable and kicks the wall, making a scuff mark with her black school Docs.

My mouth drops open. '*All* the local libraries? But . . . they can't do that, can they?'

'I think they can,' Miss Walker tells us, heading inside with us at her heels. She fills the kettle and sets out two extra mugs, opens a fresh packet of cookies.

'Libraries are closing all around the country,' she says with a sigh, making hot chocolates all round. 'Hundreds of them in the last few years . . . the figures are frightening. We've been lucky to escape this long. I don't know what will happen next, but I have a bad feeling . . . a very bad feeling!'

'It's not our fault, is it?' I check. 'The band? We did make a racket last night!'

She shakes her head. 'Nothing to do with that,' she assures us. 'It's all about money, I'm afraid.'

We sip our drinks, thoughtful.

'But . . . all those meetings!' Bex argues. 'You said everyone was determined to keep the library open!'

'Everyone except the council,' Miss Walker says. 'They're saying the building needs repair – that it's unfit for use. It's not perfect, but it's hardly derelict, is it? It looks like we're stuffed, basically . . .'

'No way!' Bex rages. 'We'll fight it all the way – we won't let this happen! They just can't!'

Miss Walker leans against the counter, shoulders sagging. 'We'll fight,' she tells us. 'We won't just roll over and let them win!'

But Bex has the shine of angry tears in her eyes, and she never cries, not ever.

I think of the letter I've just posted. Writing letters is what I do, but it seems childish now, and futile. One letter – what good can that do? It would take a lot more than that for the council to sit up and take notice. An avalanche of letters, maybe? The seed of an idea begins to grow in my mind, and the ghost of a smile lifts my spirits.

109

'We'll all help,' I say, as brightly as I can. 'We'd better run now, though. We're late for school already . . .'

'Dental appointment,' Bex says sadly, biting into another cookie.

'One last thing,' Miss Walker says. 'They're putting us on shortened hours from now on – we'll be closing at five every night. No more band practice. You'll need to find another place to rehearse. I'm sorry.'

'Don't worry,' I say. 'I'll tell the others. We'll find somewhere else. And we'll think of something to stop them, Miss Walker. We won't let the library close, I promise!'

I have no idea if it's a promise I can keep. Rescuing a library may be a step too far, even for me.

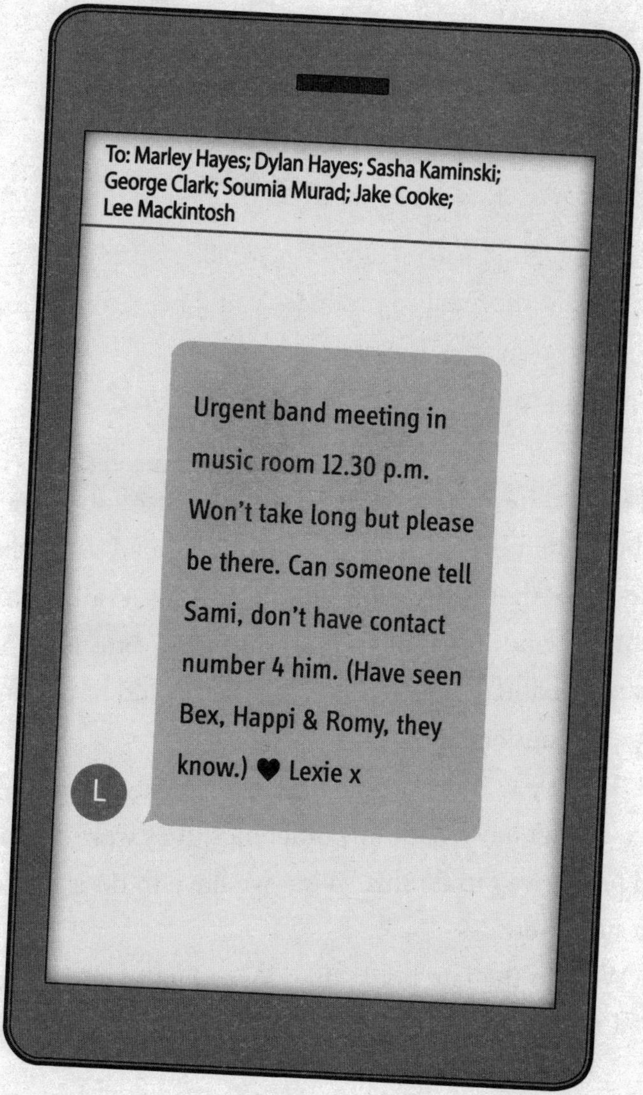
To: Marley Hayes; Dylan Hayes; Sasha Kaminski; George Clark; Soumia Murad; Jake Cooke; Lee Mackintosh
Urgent band meeting in music room 12.30 p.m. Won't take long but please be there. Can someone tell Sami, don't have contact number 4 him. (Have seen Bex, Happi & Romy, they know.) ♥ Lexie x
L

13

A Plan

'I should have gone to those stupid consultation meetings about the library,' Bex tells me as we head into school. 'I never bothered to show my face. Miss Walker said the library had tons of public support, but look what's happened! If I'd been there, maybe I could have made the council understand . . .'

'Don't you think people have been trying?' I argue. 'Bex, it wouldn't have made any difference; they were determined to find a way to do this. What we have to do is find a way to stop them.'

We sign the late book, then loiter by the noticeboard.

'I'm going to do a petition,' Bex says. 'This is serious.'

'OK,' I agree. 'We need as many ideas as we can get . . .
I'll text everyone to meet at lunchtime, tell them we've lost
our practice space. Maybe someone will think up a way to
stop all this.'

'Maybe,' Bex says. 'In the music room? Half twelve?'

'See you then . . .'

Lee Mackintosh is playing his mournful intro to our 'Back
Then' song when I head into the music room later on with
Bex, Happi and Romy.

By that time, Bex has collected one hundred and thirteen
signatures on her hastily made petition. (OK, it's actually
her French exercise book, or was, but that's a detail. The
point is, she is very persuasive.)

Happi, whose mind works along the same lines, blagged
her way on to the computer in maths (she can wind Mr
Singh round her little finger) and managed to set up an
online petition, which is gathering names almost as fast.

Now, with the band gathered too, I can sound out my
letter-writing plan.

'What's up, boss?' Marley asks, lounging on a desk top
with his little brother, eating chips. 'Written a new song?

113

Enlisted Taylor Swift to take over from Sasha? Got us a headlining gig at Glastonbury?'

'None of those,' I say. 'I'm still in shock I wrote a song at all, I'd rather have Sasha sing than Taylor Swift any day, and I don't think we're quite at the Glastonbury stage yet. Soon, though! No, this is something that will affect us all. Remember those blokes lurking around with clipboards last night, as we were going into the library?'

'Sour-looking dudes,' Dylan says.

'That's them,' I agree. 'Well, turns out they were from the council and they're trying to shut the library. No more free practice room, no more band . . . and, worst of all, no more library!'

The others look a mixture of confused, unimpressed, angry and bored.

'Sucks about the practice room,' Marley says with a shrug. 'But we'll find somewhere else – I'll ask around. Maybe we can practise here?'

I narrow my eyes. 'For a fee, we can,' I tell him. 'I've already asked. After school hours, classrooms and halls are rented out to the public to raise funds for the school and, trust me, we can't afford it. The only way it's free is if we're

doing a school play or an after-school club or something . . .
the whole place is off-limits unless there's a teacher or a
caretaker to supervise. '

'Lunchtimes?' Sasha suggests, but I shake my head again.

'Lunchtimes here are so short . . . we'd barely have a
chance to get started before we'd have to pack up,' I point
out. 'I don't think Mr Simpson would be sympathetic about
the noise, either – it's GCSE time, remember!'

'You're right,' Marley replies. 'This is where having such
a big line-up gets awkward. We need a large hut in the
middle of nowhere with soundproof walls and hot
chocolate, squash and cookies on tap . . .'

I roll my eyes.

'I'm sure we'll find another practice space,' I say. 'With
or without the hot chocolate and cookies. You're missing
the point, Marley – we can't just let them close the library!
It's . . . well, it's *our* library!'

'You can keep it,' Marley says. 'Libraries are outdated
anyway. I get enough of books at school!'

'Not quite enough, clearly,' Bex snaps. 'Or maybe you'd
do better in your exams and be a bit more clued up on
stuff. This is not all about you, Marley Hayes!'

115

He shakes his head, laughing, but Bex is fierce once she gets started.

'You think books are outdated?' she pushes on. 'What would you prefer, Marley? A society where people only learn what their computer tells them? Where they're kept ignorant of what's going on around them, ignorant of the past, oblivious to what the government might be getting up to? Because that's the way we're heading. We'll all be too busy watching TV and playing our virtual reality computer games. We'll stop caring, stop thinking, stop asking questions. We'll just be couch potatoes, brainwashed and useless.'

'Don't hold back now, Geek Girl!' Dylan sniggers, and Bex chucks the French book full of collected signatures at him. It lands on top of his perfectly gelled quiff before sliding off on to the floor.

'Nice shot,' Marley comments. 'Bet you didn't learn that in a book . . .'

'I did, actually,' she snaps. '*A Beginner's Guide to Dealing with Irritating Little Boys*, I think it was called.'

Dylan scowls, but when Bex picks up the French book and asks him to sign the list at the back, he does it without complaint. The petition makes its way around the group, and Bex asks everyone to sign Happi's online petition too, and share it with their families.

'My mum will sign, definitely,' Romy promises. 'I borrow loads of books from Bridge Street Library for her. The library in town is good, but it's a very long walk, and we don't have the cash to spare for bus fares . . .'

'My lot'll sign too,' Jake agrees. 'My little sisters love the library. We use it loads . . .'

I fling Marley a told-you-so look, and he holds his hands up in a gesture of surrender. 'OK, OK, so some people like libraries,' he admits. 'Whatever floats your boat . . . it's a free world!'

'That's just what it's not,' I point out. 'Not for the likes of us, not once they close the libraries. C'mon, Marley! Once they close it they won't be opening it again, will they? And that nice Miss Walker who brings you hot chocolate and cookies – she'll lose her job . . .'

'Nah,' Marley argues. 'They'll just move her to another library.'

I sigh, exasperated. 'You're not listening, Marley. They're closing *all* the local libraries. And it's not like there are a whole lot of other jobs around here, huh?'

'She's right,' Lee chips in. 'My dad's out of work, and he uses the library computers for his job search every day. He'll be stuffed if it shuts . . .'

'See?' Bex tells Marley crossly. 'Just because you're only interested in fighting, flirting and playing guitar, don't think others are the same!'

She collects up the paper petition again, and Happi asks everyone to share the online version on social media with a hashtag to get it trending.

'I just wanted to tell you this as a group because it does affect us all,' I say above the rumble of chat. 'I've written a letter to the council to tell them to keep the library open. I think we should all write letters – and get our families involved . . . friends . . . neighbours. If the council just see how much we all care, they'll have to reconsider!'

'Don't hold your breath,' says Marley.

'He might be right, for once,' Bex considers. 'I'm not sure if our feelings count for all that much to the council, but if we get the local paper involved, that might help. Something to make them sit up and take notice!'

'Forget the libraries,' Marley snaps. 'We have more important things to worry about. Keep your eyes peeled for a new rehearsal space, and make sure you practise this weekend. The band comes first. We can't let this ruin things for the Lost & Found, OK?'

The bell screeches to send us to afternoon lessons, and we scramble. Marley tugs at my arm as I head out of the door, but I shake him off, annoyed. His lack of interest in the library feels like a betrayal, and I feel stupid for imagining he'd want to stick up for me.

He leans towards me and I see a fresh cut on his jaw, a row of skinned knuckles on his right hand. He's been fighting again too. Great.

'I love it when you're angry,' he whispers, and I'm glad he can't see the spots of pink that burn my cheeks as I stalk away.

Dear Men in Suits,

I know a lot more now about what you were up to at Bridge Street Library yesterday and I am gutted that you are going to close it. You might not know this, but Bridge Street has the best figures for general footfall, books lent and community groups helped of all the local libraries in Millford. It would be wrong to close it. Our band will have nowhere to practise, and our book club will have nowhere to meet, and the Over-65s bingo and the Knit & Natter and the art club and all the other groups will have to stop.

I am writing this under the desk in science, so I will keep it short, but I wanted to say that I don't think you have thought this through at all.

<u>Please</u> keep Bridge Street Library open.

Love,
Lexie x

14

A Date

From the far corner of the science lab on the third floor at school, you can see the park. It's just a tiny patch of distant green glimpsed beyond the rooftops, but it's still the park, and I look out longingly now because the sun is shining and it reminds me so much of days gone by.

We always made the most of the sunshine, Mum and I. We'd pack a basket with jam butties and orange squash and apples and head to the park. It had been a bus ride away when we lived on the Skylark Estate, but that just made it more of an adventure. We'd walk down from the bus stop and run across the grass laughing, spread our picnic shawl out beside the old bandstand. From there, you could see a big, beautiful Victorian mansion called Greystones.

'Imagine living there,' Mum would say wistfully. 'This park we're sitting in was once part of their private grounds, but they still have plenty of garden left, hidden away behind the fence. It's a funny place – just one old lady, living alone, and a load of hippy-dippy hangers on – shall we move in, Lexie? What do you think?'

'We could be princesses,' I said, because Greystones looked to me like a real live fairy-tale castle.

'Well, you're my princess, always!' Mum had laughed and hugged me close.

'Lexie? Lexie, you're dreaming!' Happi's voice cuts across my thoughts. 'That's the last bell . . . come on!'

We pick up our bags and head for the door. Jake, who's in the same science class, falls into step with us, and Bex is waiting for us in the corridor.

'Want to hang out in the park for a bit?' she asks. 'It's actually sunny for a change, and we can grab ice creams if the van's in the park. You too, Jake, if you want . . .'

'Well . . . OK . . . why not?'

Minutes later, the four of us are walking towards the school gates. The buses are pulling away and most people have gone, but I spot Marley sitting on the wall, guitar slung nonchalantly over one shoulder.

I think about asking him along to the park too, then change my mind abruptly.

'All right, guys?' he says, jumping up and wandering over. ''Fraid I'm going to have to steal Lexie off you all for a bit. Thought we'd hang out at the Leaping Llama, yeah? Go over some band stuff . . .'

I'm speechless. Where does this boy get off? He's too sure of himself by half – just jumping in, assuming I'll come with him without even asking. To my shame, I'm torn between wanting to drop everything to go with him and irritation at his cheek.

Happi and Jake look embarrassed, awkward, but Bex just curls her lip, scathing. 'So, Lexie, going to let yourself be stolen?' she taunts, and that tips the scales.

'No,' I say, firmly and clearly. 'No, I'm not. Sorry, Marley – if you want to meet up, it'll have to be another

123

day. You could try asking me, and then I can check to see if I'm free – that's usually how it works. I'm sorry – I've got plans right now.'

Marley's face falls, and I wonder for a moment if I've blown it. Will he ditch my dodgy songwriting skills and ask Sasha or Soumia to work with him instead? Will he ditch me full stop? Switch his flirty attentions to someone new? I feel better for speaking out, even so. I am not a doormat. I get to decide what I will or won't do in this life, nobody else, and, no matter how cute Marley Hayes might be, he doesn't get to boss me around.

'Is this because I'm not on board with your stupid library thing?' he is asking. 'C'mon, Lexie. The band comes first, that's all!'

'Does it?' I challenge. 'Can you play guitar OK with skinned knuckles then? Lucky it wasn't anything worse, like broken fingers. Did the band come first when you decided to get into another fight?'

'It was nothing,' Marley growls. 'Just some chancer throwing his weight about.'

'Sure,' I say with a sigh. 'Same as last time. Look, Marley, I've got to go . . .'

124

'I'll call you then,' he says, slightly sulky. 'Arrange something, maybe.'

'Yeah, you do that.'

'Oooh, burn . . .' Bex says, under her breath, but not so quietly that Marley can't hear. 'Right, guys – let's go. See you around, Marley.'

'Lexie, don't be like this,' he cuts in, catching my arm as I start to head after the others. 'Let's not fall out! What's the big deal? I'm sorry if I came over a bit . . . too sure of myself, maybe? Bossy? I didn't think. Story of my life. But I didn't mean to be rude – you know that, right?'

'I guess,' I whisper. 'Marley, I can't talk now . . .'

'When can you talk then?' he presses. 'Tomorrow? We could do something then. Saturday afternoon?'

I want to say yes. I want to say yes badly, even though this boy is almost certainly not the boy I think he is, the boy I want him to be. He's a mess, battered and bruised with a side order of rude and selfish, but I like him anyway. My traitorous heart can't quite help it. The problem is that Saturday afternoons are when I hang out with Bex and Happi – if I ditch them for Marley I will never hear the last of it.

'I can't,' I tell him. 'Sorry, Marley, I have plans already . . .'

He rakes a hand through his fringe and his blue eyes blaze at me.

'What exactly do I have to do to get a date with you, Lexie Lawlor?' he huffs. 'Sunday then? Can I see you on Sunday?'

My heart is racing. A date? I can't work out if I'm happy or sad or just plain terrified. My feelings are all churned up, a tangle of anxiety and anger. Until a week ago, I barely knew Marley Hayes . . . I am beginning to wonder if things were better that way.

'Sunday, Lexie?' he repeats. 'Please?'

'Come on, Lexie!' Bex yells from along the street. 'Hurry up!'

'That girl is bugging me,' Marley says.

'She's just looking out for me,' I tell him. 'Yes . . . maybe Sunday – that'd be cool.'

'Maybe Sunday?' he echoes. 'Lexie, you are breaking my heart. *Definitely* Sunday, OK? Four o'clock outside the Leaping Llama?'

'I'll see you then!'

I pull away from him and run after the others, and Marley calls after me to say he'll see me soon, that he'll be thinking about me.

'I think I have a date,' I say under my breath as I catch up with Happi, Bex and Jake. 'A date . . . how did that happen?'

'Cupid's arrow,' Happi says, nudging me gently as we walk. 'You did the right thing, calling him out, not letting him change your plans. He's a good-looking boy, but he's too used to having things his own way. Don't let him take you for granted.'

'I won't,' I promise.

'He has a bad rep with girls,' Jake chips in. 'You probably know that, right?'

'He's dated dozens of girls and dumped them all,' Bex reminds me. 'Plus, he's always fighting; it's like a death wish. Today he got beaten up by one of the sixth-formers – guy reckoned Marley'd been flirting with his girlfriend. He's trouble, Lexie – just sayin' . . .'

Flirting with a sixth-former's girlfriend? My heart sinks and my cheeks burn with shame. Does he like me, or is this just some kind of game to Marley? I can't work it out at all.

'I know,' I say miserably. 'Look, it's probably not an actual date. He'll just want to talk about the band and stuff, like last time. I'm not interested in him that way, honest.'

I am interested in him that way, sadly. I can't help myself.

'Whatever you say,' Bex says, exasperated. Happi just links an arm through mine and we head into the park. Ten minutes later, we're eating ice-cream cones by the lake, watching a family of swans drift about on the mirror-still water.

Talk turns to the library crisis again, and this time I'm glad of the distraction.

'We can't let them win,' Jake says. 'I'll write a letter, like you said, and get my mum and sisters to do one too . . .'

'I'm making a Twitter account right now,' Happi says, glancing up from her phone. 'I can sort an Instagram and a Facebook page too when I come over tomorrow.'

'Should we plan a protest?' I wonder. 'Occupy the library and refuse to move? Chain ourselves to the railings? How do these things work?'

'I'll find out,' Bex says. 'We need to contact the *Millford Gazette* and the radio, get the whole town talking about it . . .'

128

Happi frowns. 'The thing is . . . we all use the library, but not everyone does. A lot of people are like Marley and Dylan, they just don't get why it's such a big deal. The petitions have got everyone talking at school, but it's not all pro library. Some people think libraries are old-fashioned, that we don't need them because we have e-readers and the internet –'

'Idiots,' Bex snaps.

'Maybe,' Jake argues. 'But we have to convince people, don't we? Labelling them idiots might not be the best way to do it!'

'OK,' Bex says. 'Point taken. We have to show people that libraries matter!'

I nod. 'Yes . . . if we could actually get people into the libraries . . . let them see for themselves? We could go into primary schools and talk to the kids, get their teachers to bring them along to listen to a story and sign up for a library card.'

'Good one,' Happi agrees. 'And maybe if our protest was actually a really cool event and not just chaining ourselves to railings . . . well, it could pull people in, change their minds. Change the council's mind, even!'

We all love this idea, though we're not quite sure how to make it work. It doesn't really matter for now; we have the bones of a plan, and the rest will fall into place in time.

Bex tries approaching passers-by for signatures for the petition, but walking up to total strangers is not as easy as getting the kids at school to sign, especially when they're signing a dog-eared exercise book and not an official petition. A mum with two small children adds her name, as do an elderly couple, but most people blank Bex, and one old lady shrieks as if she is trying to steal her handbag.

I guess being accosted by a turquoise-haired teen with a pierced nose might be slightly alarming if you don't actually know Bex. Possibly even if you do.

'We need flyers,' Jake says. 'And proper printed petitions on a clipboard. We need to get people interested, because Happi's right. Not everyone cares.'

'Not everyone's into books,' I say. 'But libraries are about much more than that . . . like for us, with our band practice. I've been trying all day to think of somewhere we can practise for free and not get on anyone's nerves, but I can't. It needs to be big enough, so it can't just be a kitchen or a garden shed, and church halls and studio spaces will charge

 130

us. I hope this doesn't sink the Lost & Found before we've got properly started . . .'

Jake grins. 'About that. I might know somewhere that could work. I wasn't going to say anything, because I haven't sounded it out yet . . . but we could take a look tomorrow – see what you think?'

I blink. 'That's fantastic! Sure!'

'Where is it?' Bex wants to know.

'It's in the garden of the place where I live,' Jake says. 'Greystones. Big Gothic house looking out on the park – fancy wrought-iron gates and a huge great garden, plus all kinds of outbuildings and places that might just be perfect for us!'

'Greystones?' I echo. 'Wow! That would be awesome!'

I gaze across the park, my eyes coming to rest on a distant rooftop with ornate chimneys and masses of ivy clinging to the brickwork. Little leaded windows tucked into the eaves look down over the park, and through a stand of tall trees, newly in leaf, I glimpse a balcony and the purple haze of a climbing wisteria.

Everyone in Millford knows Greystones, but I've never met anyone who actually lives there before. The place is mysterious, romantic. Local legend says that it's some kind of modern-day hippy commune, and it is also home to Millford's one and only sort of celeb, a mad lady artist whose paintings sell for a fortune and hang in prestigious galleries all round the world.

And Mum had loved it, of course . . . the two of us would build up stories about the place, imagine what it might be like to live there. My breath catches a little at the memory and when my vision blurs a little I turn away, smiling harder.

How do you show someone why libraries
matter? What they mean? How do you
explain the magic to someone who
doesn't understand?

Library Song

I found the dreams inside the words,
I found the words inside the books,
I found the books inside a library,
And I cannot tell you just what they mean to me.

The dreams catch my soul and make me sigh,
The words fill my heart and lift me high,
The books are a ladder to the sky,
Don't take that away from me.

I found a way to paint my world with colour,
I found a path to lead me through the dark,
I found a doorway that stood ajar,
And I cannot tell you what that means to me.

The doorway opened wide for me,
I stepped through the door and I could see
A world of possibility . . .
Don't take that away from me.

Men in suits came with clipboards,
Said libraries didn't matter any more,
Said hopes and dreams belong to yesterday
And are not for the likes of me.

They slammed the door to the future shut,
Took away the ladder, threw out the books,
Trampled my dreams underfoot,
Don't even care what they've done to me.

But books unleashed a power in me,
The power of dreams, the power to see.
They cannot close our library.
Cos it belongs to you and me,
Belongs to you and me . . .

15

Greystones

The Friday-evening edition of the *Millford Gazette* is full of the news that five local libraries will close to enable money to be focused on a central hub in town. 'Libraries have failed to change with the times,' a councillor is quoted as saying. 'Our local libraries are outdated, their buildings unfit for use. Library usage is falling nationally – we need to move forward, with vision and innovation, into the future.'

Bex slams her fist down on the table, swears under her breath. I can see she wants to throw something at the wall: the chilli sauce bottle, a plate of vegetable korma, an ear-splitting roar of disgust. She grits her teeth and scowls at the newspaper.

'Channel that anger,' Mandy says gently. 'Get smart, and turn it into an energy to fight against the thing that's hurting you . . .'

'It's lies,' I say, indignant. 'They're twisting words to make it look like libraries have no place any more. Library usage is only falling because so many have already been closed!'

Jon nods. 'Make sure you have an answer for every question, every piece of misinformation,' he tells me. 'Then channel that anger, like Mandy says, and fight back . . . but gently, fairly!'

Somehow, overnight, I have written a song. Maybe it's only half a song, without the music, or maybe it's a poem, I don't know for sure, but it's something. I couldn't sleep. So many worries and questions were whirling around in my head, stuff about the library, about Marley, about the band. I went over and over the piece in the paper with its lies and twisted truths, over and over Mandy and Jon's advice. Channel the anger and fight back . . . gently, fairly.

I opened my eyes in the darkness, determined. I've lost so much already in this life . . . I am not willing to lose more, not without a fight. I put the light on and started to write.

136

I love the way the words and feelings transformed from a tangled ache of anxiety and fear into something beautiful, powerful.

Songwriting, it seems, is a kind of magic.

I wanted to text Marley straight away, send him the lyrics and see if he could add his own variety of magic to the words and bring it all to life, but he hasn't texted me and there's no way I'm making the first move. The song will have to wait until Sunday.

On Saturday afternoon, after a few back-and-forth texts, Happi, Bex, Jake and I set off for Greystones, cutting across the far corner of the park. I can't help crossing my fingers as the house comes into view again beyond the stand of trees that edge the park. This would be such a cool place to practise, and easy for everyone to get to.

'It's right by the disused railway line that runs past the park, isn't it?' Bex asks. 'Used to be one of my favourite boltholes if I was running away. Nobody really comes along there except for the occasional dog walker. You can see where the train tracks used to be, but it's all overgrown now.'

'Why were you running away?' Jake asks, curious.

Bex shrugs. 'It's just what I did when stuff went wrong,' she says. 'My stepdad was getting violent? I ran away. Mum drinking again? I ran away. By the time I came to live with Mandy and Jon, it was just my way of coping with anger. In trouble at school, row about a messy bedroom, no strawberry yoghurt at breakfast . . . easy. Just do a runner.'

'She was the queen of running away,' Happi tells him. 'But she's a reformed character now.'

'I got bored,' Bex says. 'And I realized I was lucky to have Mandy and Jon, lucky to have Lexie – even you lot. Anyway . . . whatever. From what I've seen and heard, Greystones is some sort of hippy commune – am I right?'

Jake grins. 'Well, sort of. There are a few artists and craftspeople living there in a co-operative sort of way. It's not your average place, and there are some weird old vehicles and outbuildings in the grounds . . . including something that might work for us, if they'd let us use it . . .'

'And might they?'

'Why not?' Jake says. 'It belongs to Louisa Winter. She's quite old and eccentric . . .'

'And famous,' I chip in. 'She's an artist or something, right?'

'She is,' Jake says. 'But back when she was a teenager she was also a model in New York and knew loads of awesome people. Andy Warhol did a series of screen prints of her eating an ice lolly, and a poet called Leonard Cohen wrote a song about her – and there's even a photo of her on the back of Bob Dylan's motorbike in 1965 . . .'

'Wow,' Bex says. '1960s New York, Warhol and Cohen and Dylan – how did I not know this?'

'Wow,' I echo, trying to look suitably impressed. I've heard of Bob Dylan, of course, and make a mental note to look the others up; Louisa Winter's life sounds amazing, even if it did include people I've never heard of.

Jake leads us along a quiet, curving cul-de-sac with big houses dotted along one side and a wedge of ground that is half public tennis courts and half allotments on the other. I can hear birdsong and the gentle thwack-thwack of a tennis game . . . It's one of those strange roads that makes you feel you've stepped back in time.

Halfway along, there are the big black wrought-iron gates Jake mentioned. He lifts the latch and pushes the gate open a crack, and we file in, feet crunching on gravel.

'What if someone sees us?' Happi says anxiously. 'Shouldn't we ask first?'

'I live here,' Jake reminds us. 'At least, I live in one of the flats in the west wing of the house, with my mum and my two little sisters and stepdad. He's lived here for ten years, but we only moved in at the end of last summer. Before that we lived in Chinatown in London, among other places. This is a kind of paradise compared to some of the flats we've had . . .'

He frowns, as if brushing off the memory, and I try for a moment to imagine what his story might be. Jake, Romy, Sasha, Soumia, Lee, George, Sami – even Marley and Dylan – all have stories to tell, and so far I've only seen the tiniest glimpses. Like me, they probably have secrets hidden, struggles concealed, challenges they have to face every day.

I wonder if Marley is actually right, if we are all lost in our own particular way. I push the thought of Marley away.

'Anyway,' Jake is saying. 'C'mon . . .'

We veer off along a footpath that winds through long grass filled with forget-me-nots and daisies, passing an ancient caravan parked against the ivy-clad wall, the door open to reveal a ginger cat basking in a bright patch of afternoon sun. Further over there's a big canvas yurt with a pointy roof and a crooked chimney poking out at one side, and I can see some sheds and a long wooden hut with a roof completely covered in solar panels.

'A woman called Willow lives in the caravan,' Jake says. 'And Laurel and Jack live in the hut – he makes lutes and mandolins and she's an artist. When we moved here we lived in the yurt for a bit until the new flat was ready, but a guy called Mitch lives in it now . . .'

'You lived in the yurt?' I ask, wide-eyed.

'You and your mum and your stepdad and your two sisters?' Happi checks. 'Five of you?'

Jake shrugs. 'It's bigger than it looks . . . and it was only for a few months. We were in the flat by Christmas. Everyone here is a bit . . . different. People helped out, made sure we were OK.'

I think back to Jake's first few months at school and remember a quiet boy in crumpled uniform. Why hadn't I noticed, checked he was OK? Bex would have called it interfering, Happi would have called it a rescue, but maybe it would have been friendship, pure and simple?

141

'So, my stepdad is the handyman,' Jake goes on. 'He teaches t'ai chi too . . . and Mum is learning aromatherapy massage. She can get thirty pounds an hour for that at the posh spa hotel on the edge of town . . . more if she has her own place.'

It feels as if we've stepped out of the real world with its grumpy teachers and maths tests and sour-faced men in suits. Greystones is a place where time stands still, where people do things differently.

I think of Mum with a sudden ache of regret. She would have loved it here, loved to have seen beyond the tall fence into the secret garden of the house we both once dreamed about.

I bend to pick up a fallen leaf, soft and green and supple. My fingers trace its ribs, its serrated edges, while the others walk on ahead, just out of sight through the trees.

Wherever
you are, Mum,
I hope it's
somewhere
this lovely.
Love,
    Lexie x

16

Off the Rails

I can't believe my eyes.

'This is it,' Jake is saying. 'It's quite big and nobody uses it . . .'

'Sheesh, Jake!' Bex exclaims, breaking the silence. 'This I did not expect!'

On the other side of the trees, beyond the house, there's a wild, overgrown corner of garden with a strange, narrow, elongated shed shunted up against the wall. The shed is made of maroon and cream metal sheeting with varnished wooden struts and a weirdly curving roof. It seems to be raised a few feet off the ground, and two sets of handmade wooden steps lead up to side doors at either end.

My eyes struggle to make sense of it.

'Oh, my,' I breathe. 'It's . . . it's an actual *train*!'

We are looking up at an ancient railway carriage, the kind you might see in an old Agatha Christie movie – *Murder on the Orient Express*, maybe. The carriage is huge and, though it's grimy from who knows how many winters of rain and snow and there's a little rust specked across the maroon metal sheeting, it still looks elegant. Some kind of climbing plant is clinging to the side and sneaking its way in and out of a cracked window and up towards the roof.

'It's epic, Jake,' I say. 'I love it!'

Everyone is talking at once then, asking if we can look inside, if we could seriously use it as a practice space, how it even got here in the first place. Jake reminds us that the disused railway track runs alongside the grounds. Apparently, when that line was closed back in the sixties and lots of old rolling stock was scrapped or sold off, Louisa Winter's father bought the old railway carriage and had it hauled into the grounds of Greystones. He had the inside converted so his daughter could use it as a base when she was home from New York or London or Paris, so her wild-child partying wouldn't bother anyone up at the big house.

Rescuing a railway carriage . . . that's pretty amazing.

I try to picture the scene . . . a waif-like model in an A-line minidress leaning out of the railway-carriage window to greet her arty, poetic, pop-star friends when they came to stay.

Jake bounds up the steps and unlocks the door, and we crowd behind him, eager to see inside. The carriage is dark and musty, the windows grey with dust and veiled with spider's webs, but we can see what an incredible space it is. We step out of the little hallway and into a long room lined with built-in red velvet sofas faded to a dusty pink, a kitchenette kitted out with a tiny pink electric cooker and matching sink.

Jake picks up a 1960s copy of *Vogue* from the coffee table, opening it to a glossy spread featuring a long-limbed girl with huge, kohl-rimmed eyes, her long, fox-red curls flying out behind her as she rides an old-fashioned bicycle through a rose garden. Another shot shows her feeding swans on a lake, and in another she sits on the steps of a bandstand, eating an ice-cream cone while an old-fashioned brass band in military uniform play behind her.

146

'This was photographed in the park,' Bex observes, peering over my shoulder. 'Our park! It looked a lot posher then, didn't it? Is this Louisa Winter?'

Jake nods. 'She was seventeen in those shots, I think,' he tells us. 'She's an old lady now, but she's still a force of nature.'

I run a finger down a wall of black-and-white photographs thick with dust stuck to one of the gently curving walls. There are lots of shots of doe-eyed girls with boyish pixie-cuts and boys in striped tops and donkey jackets with long hair and round, mirrored shades. Are they once-famous faces from long ago? Friends from Louisa's modelling days? I'd love to know their stories.

'Wow,' Happi says in a small voice. 'What d'you think, Lexie?'

'Awesome,' I breathe. 'There's more than enough room for us and the equipment . . . It's perfect!'

'Is there electricity?' Bex is asking, flicking an old Bakelite switch up and down uselessly. Jake says that Sheddie, his stepdad, knows all about electrics and could definitely sort something out.

'I love it,' I say.

147

It's a time capsule; apart from the decades worth of dust, it's as if the seventeen-year-old Louisa just walked out moments ago. I reach into my pocket for my mobile, then let it go again; this is too personal, too private for Instagram or Facebook.

I wander along to the end of the living area and sneak a look through the door to the bedroom, the part of the railway carriage Jake's mum wants to use as a consultation room. It has the same untouched look as the main living space, but there's something else, something I can't put my finger on.

The purple op-art coverlet is still smoothed across the double bed, a fun fur rug beside it. A clothes rail still holds a tiny green tartan minidress and an embroidered muslin smock that floats out a little in the draught from the door.

It looks perfect, except that the dressing-table mirror is badly smashed. The sight of it is shocking, as though someone has thrown a brick or a boot or a piece of furniture at the glass in a fit of anger that somehow lingers. Under the dust, ugly zigzags radiate out from a central point, but although big chunks of glass are missing from the mirror, there are no jagged shards, no sharp, bright glint of

148

powdered glass among the bottles of vintage nail polish, the perfume bottle with its little woven diffuser, the muddle of eye pencils and pastel eyeshadows. The mess was cleared away years ago, but a faint aura of violence still hangs in the air.

I feel strangely upset, shaky, but I'm drawn to the dressing table all the same. I open and close a few empty drawers, and in the last drawer I try I find a green fringed shawl and a book of Buddhist meditations. I shiver a little as I touch the embroidered wool and flick through the little book.

Without warning, I'm thinking of my mum again, emotions piling up so strongly I can scarcely breathe. Something sad happened here, something scary. I can feel it, sense it, like a knot of barbed wire in my belly.

It's as if I can see beyond the shadows, behind the cobwebs and into the past. The images are hazy, but there's a man and a woman, and the man is angry. I can hear shouting, pleading, crying, shattered glass.

I just don't understand why it all feels so personal.

17

In the Artist's Studio

'Will it do?' Jake asks, as he closes up the railway carriage again. 'What d'you think, Lexie?'

Out in the May sunshine, the strange, haunted feeling lifts away as if it never happened at all, and I focus instead on how amazing the old railway carriage is.

'Tell Louisa Winter we'll do anything,' I tell Jake, suddenly desperate for this place to be ours, for a few hours a week at least. 'We'll clean it up, paint the walls, box up all her personal stuff. We'll be respectful; we won't bother anyone. And the noise shouldn't be an issue as we'd be so far away from the house . . .'

'Tell her yourself,' Jake says, and, before I can protest, he tugs my arm and I'm walking with him up to the house. Bex and Happi hang back on the path, in theory so as not to overwhelm Miss Winter, but in practice because it's a slightly weird situation and nobody is quite sure how to approach it.

Jake rings the bell. It echoes through the house, clanging and ominous. Moments later the door swings open and there is Louisa Winter.

She is tiny, a slender figure in a long linen art smock smudged and streaked with oil paint. She's elderly, of course, with laughter lines around her red lipsticked mouth and feathery crow's feet radiating out from startling jade-green eyes. Most amazing of all is her hair, a messy tangle of blazing auburn dragged back from her face, secured with a tortoiseshell clip and speared through with a couple of paintbrushes that stick out at alarming angles.

I've never seen such a striking woman. She might not be young, but she has style and attitude by the bucketload. She manages to look somehow fierce and other-worldly at the same time.

152

'Jake?' she says, then her gaze moves to me. 'And . . . do I know you, young lady? You look *very* familiar, but I can't quite place you . . . Perhaps it's just that you remind me of someone? Have we met?'

'I don't think so,' I say, as brightly as I can. 'My name is Lexie Lawlor. I was born in Scotland, but I've lived here since I was nine . . .'

'Ah, just my old eyes playing tricks,' she says. 'Take no notice of me. So, Jake and Lexie, what can I do for you?'

'Ms Winter,' Jake begins politely, 'I wondered if you could help us? My friends and I are in a band, and we've been practising in the meeting room at Bridge Street Library. Lexie here is one of the songwriters . . . she's very talented. The others too . . .'

He gestures vaguely at Happi and Bex, who wave awkwardly from the path.

Jake ploughs on. 'But now they're closing the library . . .'

Louisa Winter frowns. 'Fools,' she snaps. 'I saw it in the newspaper. What are they thinking of? They'll be burning books next, and we all know where that leads. Anarchy. Chaos. Wickedness. The death of culture!'

I bite my lip, a little alarmed at the thought.

153

'I think it's wrong,' I blurt out, clumsily. 'We're trying to stop them, but I don't think they'll listen to us . . .'

Louisa Winter tilts her head to one side, thoughtful.

'Look, you'd better come in,' she says. 'I was just about to put the kettle on. Come along – all of you. Don't skulk there on the path!'

Bex and Happi run up the steps and the four of us enter the hallway, closing the heavy door behind us. Louisa Winter strides away, her ancient lace-up boots tap-tapping on the tiled floor. We follow her into a big, cluttered studio, flooded with light and filled with easels, canvases, tables strewn with brushes and tubes of paint. An outsized Swiss cheese plant jostles for space with a giant tribal shield, a huge, age-speckled mirror and a vintage-shop mannequin draped in red velvet; two paint-stained antique sofas are boxed in by stacks of paintings in various stages of completion.

'Wow,' I whisper, breathing in the smell of turps and oil paint and linseed oil along with the aura of mystery. 'Just . . . wow!'

'It's a privilege to see your studio, Ms Winter,' Happi says, always the most polite. 'I've seen one of your paintings

154

before, in the art gallery in town. It was amazing. The one of the woman holding a fox.'

'That's right,' Louisa Winter says. 'I'm glad you liked it. And you are?'

'Happi,' she says. 'This is Bex.'

'Well, let's get the kettle on and find some mugs, shall we?' Louisa Winter says. 'Jake, you'll find tea and milk and sugar on the counter over there; biscuits too, I think. If you could bring them all over and rinse a few mugs so there's enough for everyone. Sit down, girls. Make yourselves at home.'

We squash awkwardly on the sofas, balancing mugs of dark brown tea and clutching iced biscuits, our eyes scanning the studio, taking everything in. I've never seen the painting in the art gallery, the one Happi mentioned, but I can see half a dozen paintings now and they're incredible. Louisa Winter seems to specialize in big canvases depicting stylized people and animals. The paintings look mystical, timeless; the women doe-eyed and trance-like. Ivy twines round the arms of the woman in the painting closest to me, snaking its way up through her hair.

Louisa Winter perches at the end of one sofa, sipping her tea from a vintage china cup. 'So,' she says. 'Was it just

155

the library you wanted to talk about, or is there something else?'

'It's kind of linked,' Jake explains. 'Bridge Street Library is shutting early from now on, so our band has nowhere to practise. We're looking for somewhere big enough; somewhere we won't get in the way. Sheddie mentioned that you'd asked him to do up the old railway carriage so Mum and Willow could use one of the rooms as a holistic treatment centre . . .'

'And you thought you'd use it for band practice too?' Louisa Winter asks. 'I see. Are you saying you could share that space? Plan out times to use it?'

Jake shrugs. 'Mum and Willow only want to use the bedroom bit anyway, for aromatherapy massage and reflexology and stuff. There's a door at that end too, and a little hallway that could act as a waiting room. The two parts of the railway carriage can be totally separate if we keep the connecting door closed . . . It's no problem as long as we don't practise when they've got clients. We could definitely make it work!'

'Well, if there's only four of you . . .' the old lady muses.

'Um, twelve, actually,' I say bravely. 'It was kind of hard to exclude anyone. And we have an amazing sound – trumpet, violins, cello, keyboard, flute and the usual drums and guitar, obviously.'

'Obviously,' Louisa Winter says. 'Twelve people? My goodness! It sounds . . . very interesting. What do you play, Jake?'

'The triangle,' he says, deadpan. 'Well, no . . . I don't play anything, I am more of the tech guy, really. Or the publicist. Or the roadie, maybe. We'll be no trouble, Ms Winter – you'll hardly know we've been there!'

'Ha! I've heard that one before,' she says. 'A few people have stayed there on and off over the years . . . Ked Wilder was here a lot, of course. David hid here for a week to do some songwriting and scandalized the locals by wandering about the park in a maxi dress . . .' Her eyes shine, lost in memories of long ago, and then she blinks and shakes her head.

'Lots of people popped in and out, but not for a while now,' she muses. 'I did a favour for a friend's daughter, ten or fifteen years ago, and . . . let's just say it didn't work out. I suppose you can use it – you seem like nice enough kids.

You'll have to look after it, or the deal is off. It needs clearing out and painting. I've talked to Sheddie about that. But why not? It'll be good to have some young people about the place again, some music.'

'Would there be a charge?' Bex asks. 'A rent?'

'Of course not! Why would I want to take your money? Always supposing you have any.'

'We don't,' Happi says. 'That's the problem.'

'Not to me,' the old lady says. 'Use the place, just don't wreck it . . .'

'Is that a yes?' I check. 'Really?'

Louisa Winter laughs. 'It's a yes,' she says.

Dear Mum,

I have so much to tell you. I've written another song . . . about libraries this time. I used to love going to the library with you, you know. I remember every one, from the big Victorian library when we lived in Edinburgh to the library bus that came to our village every week and all the ones in between. You never came to Bridge Street Library – we used the one on the Skylark Estate, but that's closing too, and anyone who knows the Skylark knows that the library is probably the best place there.

I wish you were here to sign your name on the petition Bex has made.

I wish you were here to give me some advice about boys too. It's something we never talked about – you never mentioned my dad and you never seemed to have any other boyfriends, and I haven't had a crush on a boy since I was seven years old and fell in love with Daniel Radcliffe in the Harry Potter films.

This is different. I think about him all the time (not Daniel Radcliffe – the boy) but now he's asked me on an actual date I'm terrified. I don't think I'm ready for it. This boy is good-looking and funny and clever and kind, but he can be thoughtless and vain as well. He has a bad rep at school for getting into fights all the time, and he's had tons of girlfriends. Everybody says he's trouble. I know I should stay away but I think sometimes my heart will break if I can't have him.

Mandy and Jon are calling me . . . They've lit the fire pit and we're having baked potatoes and barbecued veggie kebabs, and I'm going to put this letter into the flames so it turns to ash and flies up into the air and reaches you that way, wherever you might be. Maybe.

Boys are very confusing. Is it normal to feel so mixed up? I wish I could ask you, Mum.

The big date is tomorrow, so wish me luck.

Love,
Lexie x

18

Marley Brings Flowers

Marley Hayes is standing outside the Leaping Llama Cafe with his guitar slung over his shoulder and a bunch of bluebells in his hand. The flowers are wilting a little, the violet-blue blooms bowing their heads sadly, but nobody has ever given me flowers before, not ever, and bluebells are my absolute favourite.

This is my first real date. I spent hours getting ready, trying on every piece of clothing I own in the quest to look cool, careless, confident. In the end I settled for a red swishy skater skirt and a long-sleeved black T-shirt, swiping eyeliner beneath my lashes to create the perfect cat's eye flick. I wish it were as easy to make sense of my tangled feelings.

I watch Marley for a full five minutes from across the street, half hidden behind a tree, telling myself that, no matter what kind of a bad rep he has, things could still be different for us. Is that optimism or just plain stupidity? When I look at Marley's blue eyes anxiously scanning the street, I somehow don't care. I cross the street and say hello.

'These are for you,' he says as I approach, holding out the flowers. 'They've gone a bit sad-looking . . . sorry!'

'They're perfect,' I say.

We head into the Leaping Llama, order hot chocolates and slide into a corner booth. 'I'm trying to make this a proper date experience,' Marley says. 'Flowers and hot chocolate and maybe dinner – you can't say I'm not trying!'

'Very trying,' I quip.

'Still mad at me?'

I sigh. 'I wasn't mad at you, Marley, just . . . just a bit hurt about the libraries thing and a bit embarrassed at the way you got all bossy in front of my friends.'

He peers at me from beneath his fringe, blue eyes penitent. 'Look, I'm an idiot sometimes. I know I was a bit

 162

full of myself, expecting you to drop everything. I'm too used to getting my own way!'

Marley drops an unlikely three spoonfuls of sugar into his drink, stirring it grimly. 'Plus . . . the fight thing. You're not impressed, are you?'

'Impressed?' I echo. 'No, Marley, I'm not impressed that you get yourself beaten up at regular intervals. It's kind of weird. Word has it that the fight kicked off because you were flirting with some sixth-form girl . . .'

'Are you jealous?' he asks, eyes alight. 'Because you don't need to be, Lexie. She's just a friend . . .'

'I'm not jealous,' I lie. 'Why should I care?'

Marley looks hurt then, and I'm the one left feeling bad. It's kind of awkward, as if both of us are suddenly shy. I wonder again if I want to get involved with a boy who likes fighting and never wins, who flirts with everything in a skirt, who veers dangerously between charming, rude and selfish and unexpectedly vulnerable.

'Give me a chance, Lexie,' he says now. 'I'll pack in the fighting if that will make you happy. I'll do whatever you want!'

'I just want you to be yourself,' I say, exasperated. 'Right now I can't work you out at all!'

'Be myself? You might not like the real me,' Marley says. 'Not many people do. Suppose the real me is rude and vain and ruthless? Or sick, pathetic, disgusting scum? I've been called all those things.'

I blink, shocked.

'Might be some truth in the first few,' I counter. 'Rude . . . sometimes, yes. Vain . . . probably. Ruthless? I haven't seen that side of you yet, but I can believe it's there. I'm not sure about those last labels, though. Who called you those things? An ex girlfriend? You must have been way out of line . . .'

'Nah, not an ex,' he says, his eyes drifting away from me to gaze out of the window. 'They tend to be kinder, funnily enough. It was my dad. Those are some of the nicer words he has for me . . . Let's just say we don't get on.'

I asked for the real Marley Hayes and I'm getting it now – perhaps more real than I bargained for.

'I'm sorry,' I say. 'That sucks.'

'It does,' he agrees, still staring into the distance. 'My dad's not a nice bloke. A bit too handy with his fists. He has good taste in music – Bob Marley and Bob Dylan, hence the names, but those are the only good things he ever gave us.'

I slide my hands across the table towards Marley, and he holds them tight. His palms feel warm and strong, and his skin is tanned against my own, still winter-pale. My heart is thumping.

'My dad's a loser,' Marley says. 'If I'm a bit messed up, blame him. Like I said, we're all a bit lost, right? We all have secrets, stuff we hide.'

Marley is being honest, I know that because I can feel his discomfort at showing so much of himself. He's trying to be real, but instinct tells me that what I'm seeing is still just the tip of the iceberg.

What else are you hiding, Marley? I wonder, but it's something I can't bring myself to ask.

'I like you, Lexie,' he says. 'I know people at school think I'm a user. I have a terrible track record with girls. But I really think we could be different. We could!'

'I don't know,' I admit truthfully. 'Everybody's warned me against you . . .'

'Do you care?' he asks, and suddenly it really is that simple. Do I care what other people think? I don't think I do, not any more.

'I don't care,' I tell him. 'I just want to know the real you.'

165

He's laughing now. 'You have no idea, Lexie Lawlor, he says. 'Seriously, you don't. But I don't care either, OK? I like you more than I've liked anyone in ages. You're clever and talented and you call me out on stuff when I get too full of myself. I'll try not to be such a loser the next time I see you with your friends. I was out of order, and I'm sorry. Can you tell?'

'I think I can . . .'

'Well, in case you're not certain, listen to this,' he says. 'I wrote a song for you, and I've never actually written a song for a girl before! Want to hear it?'

He takes out his guitar, back in his comfort zone again. Pushing his chair back, he begins to play, a rolling, bittersweet melody that's managing to break my heart even without any words. It's wonderful . . . and it's mine.

'Can you write some words for it?' Marley asks, the moment the last chord dies away. 'Our song!'

I frown. 'Sure, only I don't know the story yet. I only know how it begins, not how it ends.'

'Who said it was going to end?' he demands. 'We could be the greatest love story of the modern age! The Romeo and Juliet of the twenty-first century!'

 166

'I hope not,' I say. 'Romeo and Juliet both topped themselves, y'know . . .'

'OK, OK, forget them,' he says. 'Let's just be ourselves: Marley and Lexie! So what'll we do now? Something fancy? Cinema? Bag of chips? This is supposed to be the perfect date, remember!'

'Well, there's something I want to show you!'

I tell Marley about Greystones and the old railway carriage. His confidence crumbles, his eyes flashing hurt, and suddenly I'm treading carefully again.

'You didn't tell me,' he says. 'You didn't want me with you to check it out?'

'It was a bit awkward after Friday,' I say. 'I thought I'd scope it out first.'

Marley sighs. 'I guess. I mean, it sounds good – I've been so scared that the Lost & Found was going to fizzle out before it even properly begins . . .'

'Not if I can help it,' I promise.

And right there, in the booth at the Leaping Llama, he leans over, pulls me close and kisses me.

Just...wow.
Seriously.

L x

19

A Long-Lost Legend

I hand my library song lyrics over to Marley as we sit on the steps of the old railway carriage later that night.

'You wrote me a song too?' he checks, wide-eyed. 'That's amazing!'

'I wrote it for the library,' I tell him. 'But . . . well, I wondered if you could do anything with it. Make it into something.'

He scans the words.

'I really did put my foot in it on Friday, didn't I?' he says. 'Dylan and me, we're not big into books and reading. Just never got the habit, and books seem like a chore, somehow. Like work.'

'That's because you only read for school,' I point out. 'Libraries are all about reading what you want to read, for fun or for research. Books on musicians, maybe?'

'Maybe,' he says. 'Never thought of that. Anyway, I was out of order shooting my mouth off like that. I'll make some music for your song, Lexie. It'll be a challenge to work this way round!'

'I'll work on your song too,' I promise. 'Our song. Whatever!'

'C'mon,' he says with a grin. 'Back to work!'

We'd abandoned all hope of a proper date to come straight here, and Marley fell in love with the place, just as I knew he would. Already, someone – Jake, maybe – has made a start on packing up the vintage magazines and peeling the old photos off the wall, but the magic still hangs in the air, so real you can almost touch it.

Marley discovers a broken Dansette record player and a cupboard full of vinyl records from the sixties, lots of them signed. 'Have you seen this?' he asks, over and over. 'I mean this is treasure! The Beatles, The Stones, The Kinks, David Bowie, Ked Wilder – all these amazing oldies! Must be worth a fortune!'

I pick up a Ked Wilder single, wiping a layer of dust from its sleeve to see more clearly the legendary sixties pop hero with his mop of black hair, skinny jeans and dodgy winklepicker shoes. He stayed here lots of times, according to Miss Winter. I try not to wonder which other long-gone performers have been right here in this room, writing songs or partying or just taking some time out. The magic still lingers, somehow.

We spend the rest of our date night clearing the main living space of personal stuff, boxing it up for Jake to take up to the house. With the valuables gone, we're left with worn-out rugs, peeling paint, faded couches and windows thick with dirt.

'It's a mess,' Marley says. 'But it's a beautiful mess, right?'

It really is.

The next week is crazy. Almost every spare moment is spent down at the old railway carriage. Most of the band get involved, though Romy can't stay late – she says her mum's not well – and Sami doesn't show his face at all. Marley says that his uncle and aunt are strict, and don't quite understand what this is all for.

 171

'Sami lives with his uncle and aunt?' I ask.

Marley stares at me. 'You don't know about Sami?' he says. 'Seriously? He's from Syria, Lexie. A refugee. He lost his whole family on the journey over, but he got to come to Britain as an unaccompanied minor because he had relatives here. I thought everyone knew?'

'Not me,' I whisper. 'Oh, Marley, how awful!'

To lose your mum is bad. What must it feel like to lose your whole family? To pitch up alone in a strange country thousands of miles from home? No wonder his eyes are dark with shadows. No wonder his flute playing makes the hairs on the back of my neck stand on end.

That's the moment when I know for certain that the Lost & Found is not just about music but much, much more, and I'm grateful to Marley for railroading me into doing something way outside my comfort zone. How many of the others are grateful too? Awkward, overweight Romy, for sure; shy, bespectacled George; ambitious, determined Soumia; and beautiful Sasha with her eyes full of secrets.

On Monday night we clean, a whole squad of us with mops and buckets and dusters. Lee provides trumpet

172

backing while the rest of us work, and it is strangely satisfying.

On Tuesday, we wallpaper the railway carriage with sheet after sheet of old music, the pages overlapping to make a beautiful patchwork. The sheet music is from a box I rescued not long ago; this is the perfect use for it.

On Wednesday, we throw out the moth-eaten rugs and paint the old floorboards. Jake's stepdad, Sheddie, tells him he can take his pick of the leftover emulsion paint in one of the old workshops, so we carry the whole lot up to the train and begin to paint thick, swirling stripes, pale golden yellow, tulip red and sky blue.

'What will Miss Winter think?' Happi asks, anxious. 'This is probably not what she had in mind!'

'She lived through the sixties,' Bex reminds us. 'Psychedelia and all that crazy stuff. She won't bat an eyelid!'

'Apparently the *Millford Gazette* called round to interview her today,' Jake comments. 'And she kept them on the topic of the library closures the whole time. It should go in on Friday . . .'

'That's handy,' Bex says. 'I'm taking the petitions to town on Saturday afternoon. I've printed out some official-looking ones and borrowed a couple of clipboards from school. If the newspaper interview is good, we should get lots more people wanting to sign!'

'Me and Lexie have been working on something else that might help the library campaign,' Marley says with a wink in my direction. 'It's almost ready. Can we get Sasha along tomorrow? A snare drum, a violin or two? There's a new song we need to try out!'

On Thursday, Happi, Bex, Jake and I carry on with the rainbow swirls while Marley plays us some guitar riffs and Sasha tries to fit the words to the music. Working together makes the song a genuinely joint effort, and what started out as my own private reaction to the library closures looks like it could be our next song.

On Friday, the railway carriage is off-limits while Jake's stepdad sorts out the electrics, checks that the tiny bathroom is working properly, and sands and varnishes the woodwork. We take the evening off, and it just happens to be the evening that Louisa Winter's interview appears in the *Millford Gazette*.

It's not just one page – it's a full-colour centre spread! I open it up on the living-room carpet and Mary Shelley

174

mooches over to take a look. 'National Treasure Louisa Winter Condemns Library Carnage,' the headline blares. There's a big colour picture of Louisa posing next to one of her paintings, artist's palette in hand, her green eyes gazing at the camera. On the opposite page there are older photos of Louisa in her modelling days, including one of her hand in hand with sixties pop legend Ked Wilder. I begin to read.

> Millford's very own Louisa Winter, internationally acclaimed artist, sixties wild-child and modelling sensation has spoken out about the imminent closure of five local libraries. Speaking from her Millford studio, Louisa likened the closures to 'throwing our children's futures away and making a bonfire of all we have learned about culture, community, education and creativity'.

My mobile buzzes into life with an incoming call from Jake.

'Have you seen it?' he demands, breathless. 'In the paper? Louisa's interview?'

'I'm reading it now,' I say. 'It's good! She says she's getting all her famous friends to write letters to the council, and I bet loads of people locally will write their own now!'

'Have you got to the bit about the festival?' Jake asks. 'Keep reading, Lexie. Louisa says we're having a big festival in the park in June to protest about the cuts and the closures. Everyone's invited along to support the libraries, and local bands are invited to perform . . .'

'That could be us!' I exclaim. 'June's a bit too soon, really, but –'

'We're doing it,' Jake interrupts. 'We have to, because Louisa's told the paper we're playing.' He reads aloud:

Newly formed local teen band the Lost & Found will play support for sixties pop legend Ked Wilder, who often stayed in Millford at the height of his fame and was a regular at Bridge Street Library. The festival will be Wilder's first public performance in more than a decade and is expected to draw a crowd of thousands.

'You're *kidding*,' I say, and then I find it in the newspaper spread before me and my eyes widen. 'Whoa – you're not kidding! Jake, this is awesome. And terrifying. And . . . what are we going to do?'

'I'll ring the others,' he tells me. 'You tell Bex and Marley.'

I click to end the call. Mary Shelley stalks across the newspaper and stops to look at me, inscrutable, her beaky little face tipped to one side. I think she's trying to be encouraging. It's difficult when your best friend is a tortoise . . . conversation can be kind of one-sided.

I scan though the interview again, trying to take it all in.

'Bex!' I yell. 'Quick! We're going to be famous!'

Dear Mum,

You will not believe what has happened. We've only been a band for two weeks, and now we've got a gig supporting a very famous 1960s pop star ... It would be exciting if it wasn't so scary. Anyway, it's Ked Wilder — do you remember him? I know he was well before your time, and he'll be ancient now, but it's still a massive thing because he's like the king of British pop and he hasn't played live for more than ten years, so lots of people will turn out to see him. And they'll see us too, which is the scary bit.

I'm getting on OK with M (The Boy). He hasn't kissed me again — is that normal? Maybe I was rubbish and put him off ... Bex says I have to be strict and tell him to keep his hands to himself, but he isn't like that at all. He's quite romantic, though. He's written the music for a song for me, and I have to write the words. It's difficult because I'm not sure what our story is yet, and everything I try just comes out wrong.

I wish you were here to ask. I miss you more than ever.

Love,
Lexie x

20

Going Places

It's Saturday morning and Marley is like a kid at Christmas. He's so excited at the idea of the festival that he is driving me crazy, talking non-stop and grabbing my hands every few minutes to dance me around in some kind of celebration dance. This is not ideal when you're trying to walk along the street, trust me. People tend to stare.

I am marching him over to Bridge Street Library to sign him up for a library card; he's so grateful about the whole library protest thing that he's actually agreed.

'Stop it, Marley!' I say, laughing, pulling away from him now. 'Calm down!'

'Calm down?' he echoes. 'You're kidding, right? I can calm down when I'm dead, but right now I am *buzzing*! We've got our first gig and it's going to be *huge*. Supporting Ked Wilder – do you have any idea what that means?'

I roll my eyes. 'Five solid weeks of hard work and slog followed by half an hour of sheer terror, that's what it means,' I tell him. 'We're nowhere near ready for this, Marley! We only have one song, and even that's rough around the edges!'

'Two songs,' he corrects me. 'That library thing will be top of our playlist. Have you managed to do anything with the guitar piece I wrote for you?'

'I haven't had time,' I argue. 'I've been scrubbing cobwebs off windows and painting psychedelic stripes all week, remember? And then there was the small distraction of school! Give me a chance!'

'A chance?' Marley says. 'I'd give you my heart on a platter, Lexie Lawlor. You are awesome. This gig – it's all thanks to you. You found us a new practice space – one we can use every evening if we want to – and you found us Louisa Winter, who just so happens to be

180

rich, famous and very well connected. Oh, and as loopy about libraries as you are! Don't worry, I'm not knocking it . . .'

'Good,' I say. 'And it's Jake we have to thank, anyway. He lives at Greystones; he's the one who found Louisa!'

Marley shrugs. 'Whatever . . . Look, I admit I was wrong. You were right. Libraries open doors. Who knew?'

'I knew,' I remind him, grinning.

'OK, OK, rub it in why don't you . . .'

Inside the library, it's even busier than usual for a Saturday. Miss Walker is looking extra cool in a vintage style dress printed with shelves of books. 'My library dress,' she says, giving a little twirl. 'I am fighting this every inch of the way, and every which way I can!'

She hands us the form for Marley to fill out for his library card, plus an extra one to take back for Dylan, and when I explain about our plan to get as many people to sign up as possible she smiles and tells us that lots of people have been in during the week to do just that.

'As for today, it's been non-stop!' she says. 'It's not even lunchtime, and already I've had the *Millford Gazette* in asking how I feel about the library closures – and would you

181

believe that Radio Millford are calling in five minutes to do a live round-up of what's happening? Miss Winter's interview has certainly stirred things up a bit!'

'That's brilliant!'

'It is,' she agrees, putting Marley's information into the computer. 'The radio researcher asked if any of the protesters were available to chat, and in walk you two! Could you say a few words about why you care so much about Bridge Street Library and how the whole protest festival idea came about?'

'Yesss!' Marley crows. 'How cool? We're going to be on the radio!'

My reaction is less gleeful. 'Um . . . I'm not sure I can,' I tell Miss Walker. 'I think Bex might speak better than either of us.'

'Bex isn't here and you are,' the librarian points out. 'Please, Lexie? For the libraries? It's nothing scary, just a little chat on the phone . . .'

'A chat on the phone with half the town listening in,' I say, and then the penny drops – people really are out there listening. Speaking out might help the libraries, but more than that, someone might recognize my name and find a way to contact my mum. I just need to say who I am and mention that I'm in foster. It has to be worth a shot, surely?

'We'll do it, no worries,' Marley is saying. 'Might be fun . . .'

Another librarian, the plump, grey-haired one, comes over to hold the fort at the desk while the interview takes place, and then the telephone rings. Miss Walker picks it up, smiling and nodding at us, and we know right away she's talking to a researcher and isn't actually live on air, because she gives our names and explains who we are. The researcher talks to each of us in turn, to check we're coming over loud and clear – or possibly to make sure we're not nuts.

'Don't think of it as radio,' she says. 'Imagine you're talking to a friend. We're just coming to the end of the traffic report – Tony will be with you soon! Can you put Miss Walker back on the line?'

The whole library is hushed as the clock shows it's twelve, and Miss Walker's face lights up as she begins to chat, telling listeners about the busy library and how upset her regulars are that it will soon be closing. She invites anyone who

183

thinks that libraries are old-fashioned to call in and see for themselves.

'The council tell us that kids today don't use libraries, but that's absolutely not the case here,' she declares. 'In fact, some of our most passionate protesters are teens. I'm handing over to Lexie Lawlor, a thirteen-year-old from the local school who can tell you herself just why she cares so much . . .'

Miss Walker hands the telephone to me. She has already given me the best and clearest introduction possible. If anyone out there is looking for me, they'll know I'm safe, at least.

'Hello, Lexie!' the presenter says brightly. 'The media would have us believe that teenagers are too wrapped up in themselves to care about things like libraries; is that true? Tell us how you got involved in speaking up for Millford libraries!'

Marley digs me in the ribs, and I stumble out of silence.

'Well, me and my foster sister Bex have been using Bridge Street Library for years,' I begin. 'Miss Walker runs some cool reading groups and we get to have hot chocolate and cookies . . .'

I'm wandering off the point, but the presenter doesn't seem to mind.

'Hot chocolate, eh?' he says. 'If only all libraries were like that!'

'Libraries are not just about books these days,' I point out. 'Although the books are vital because we don't have a library at school any more, and not everyone has books or Kindles at home. Libraries do other things too, though – there are lots of groups that meet here. My friends and I are in a band and we used to practise here, but now that the libraries are being closed we'll have nowhere to go. We're all upset, because actually the libraries belong to us and the council shouldn't be allowed to take them away or sell them off or whatever. My mum used to take me to libraries loads when I was little. Those were brilliant times. The council should be supporting libraries, not slamming the doors shut!'

'Well said, Lexie!' the presenter booms. 'Now I believe your friend Marley is going to tell us all about this protest festival? Welcome to the show, Marley Hayes!'

Marley takes the phone and chats away with charm and confidence, skirting around the fact that the first he knew

185

of the protest festival was when I called last night to say I'd read about it in the paper. To hear him tell it, he'd pleaded with Louisa Winter to get involved, and she'd agreed, rewarding his determination with a debut slot at the festival.

'My girlfriend and co-writer Lexie has collaborated with me on a song for the libraries,' he states. 'We're a new band, but let's just say that Louisa Winter and Ked Wilder have taken a very keen interest in our work . . .'

I raise my eyebrows, amazed at his cheek, but Marley just grins and shrugs, unrepentant. By the end of his interview, he's wangled us an invitation to showcase our songs on air once the festival is over.

Marley hands the phone back to Miss Walker, and I drag him over to the library's music section. I stand him in front of the biographies and watch his mouth drop open.

'If you want tips on how to make it in the music business, this is where to find them,' I whisper as he flicks through a book about the Red Hot Chili Peppers. 'Although, judging by that performance, you're pretty much a pro already. What was all that about pleading with Louisa Winter? You've never even met her!'

186

'It made a better story,' he says. 'I got us a showcase slot for after the festival, didn't I?'

'You did,' I agree. 'But what if we're not ready by then, Marley? What if we're rubbish, or if we can't write any more songs? What if we can't play the festival, let alone the showcase? It's a lot of pressure for a new band, especially with half of us struggling to get permission to come out to practise!'

He pulls a face. 'Don't you want us to succeed?' he asks.

'Of course I do!' I say with a sigh. 'That's the whole point! We need to be realistic. It's going to take a *lot* of hard work to get to the point where we can play in public.'

'So we'll do that hard work,' Marley declares. 'That's all there is to it!'

In the end, he chooses a biography of Ked Wilder so he can research the man we'll supposedly be sharing a stage with. 'I want to impress him,' he says simply.

'You can borrow more than one book, y'know,' I say, and Marley laughs out loud and tells me not to push it, which is probably fair enough.

The radio interview is over now, and Miss Walker hands Marley his library card and checks out his book.

187

'You guys were amazing,' she tells us. 'So natural, Lexie! And, Marley, you were awesome!'

'Don't tell him that!' I wail. 'He'll start to believe it!'

We're on our way again, heading for town to scour the charity shops for rugs and throws for the old railway carriage.

Marley slips his hand in mine as we walk.

'I'm awesome,' he whispers in my ear. 'Stick with me, kid – we're going places!'

Going Places

I met a boy who laughed and touched my hand
And woke me from the longest sleep.
He spread his wings and told me we could soar
If only I was brave enough to leap.

Chorus: We're going places, you and I,
     This boy said to me.
     We're going places, we can fly,
     Spread your wings, be free.

I met a boy who kissed me, touched my heart,
Made promises of dreams I couldn't see.
Behind him lay a trail of tears, but still
I thought it would be different, him and me.

Chorus

I met a boy who told me to be brave,
Who led me to a clifftop, tall and steep.
He took my hand and we began to run,
Raced to the very edge and made our leap.

Chorus

He soared, borne up by hope and luck and dreams,
But when I jumped I fell out of the sky.
I'm falling, lost again and lonely,
And he is up there now, still flying high.

21

Famous for Fifteen Minutes

I'd go to the ends of the earth for Marley Hayes and, yes, I'd probably jump off a cliff for him too. Not an actual cliff, obviously, but the point is that I'd risk a lot if he asked me to. I think about him all the time, dream about him the way I once dreamed of Daniel Radcliffe from the Harry Potter films.

I'm just not sure he feels that way about me.

He's sweet, he's funny, he's endlessly flirty, but if I needed him, would he be there for me? I honestly don't know. Bex has warned me over and over that Marley never sticks with a girl for more than two weeks – maybe my time is up?

My mum walked away from me; now I've chosen a boyfriend who might do the same. Fear of being abandoned all over again seeps through my veins like poison, waking me up at night.

As for the song lyrics, I can't tell if they're actually about Mum or Marley.

How do you tell the boy who wrote a piece of music for you that the words you've written for it tell a sad story, one with no happy ending? I hand him my notebook lyrics and the GarageBand link on my mobile as we sit together on the railway carriage steps, waiting for the others to show up for Monday's band practice – our first proper one since being evicted from the library.

'I'm not saying this is our story,' I tell him. 'It's just a story that came into my head randomly. I've been stuck for ages, trying to think of something, and I know you needed it done, so . . . is this OK? You did inspire it, kind of, when you mentioned "going places" the other day.'

Marley looks at the lyrics and listens to my rough-cut sung version for a second time, and his mouth curves into a smile.

'It's good,' he says. 'I think it could be our best yet. But we'd better stop calling it "our song" in case we end up

191

doomed to live out the story. I am gonna fly high, y'know –
but I'm taking you with me, Lexie Lawlor!'

He pulls me close and leans in for a kiss. My heart starts
to race and I close my eyes and part my lips, but at the last
moment he veers away and kisses my nose, laughing. I open
my eyes abruptly and laugh too, but a part of me feels hurt,
rejected. It's more than a week since Marley first kissed me,
and that was when he last kissed me too. Aren't boys –
especially boys like Marley – supposed to be mad for
all that?

'Watch him,' Bex had told me, before that first date.
'He's going to push his luck, stands to reason – be strict
with him!'

But I haven't needed to be strict. There has been no lip
action at all since the cafe, and I am convinced that means
I am a rubbish kisser. I probably am, being so new to it and
all, but how am I supposed to improve if he won't come
near me? How am I supposed to know what I'm doing
wrong?

Before I have time to worry much more, Jake, Bex and
Happi come wandering across the grass and we head inside.
The railway carriage looks incredible now. The faded bench

192

sofas are draped in bright blankets found on Saturday's charity-shop hunt and Dylan's battered old drum kit sits in pride of place at the end of the room. Marley says he plans to keep it here from now on, that this might actually prevent a lot of family arguments.

Happi sets a tin of traybakes on the kitchen counter while I set the kettle to boil, making hot drinks for anyone who wants them. By the time I've handed out the mismatched mugs, everyone is here, setting up, tuning up, admiring the finished space and running through their pieces in a cacophony of music and chat.

'Are we ready?' Marley yells above the noise. 'I hope you all like our new practice space – a big thanks to everyone who's helped us get it cleaned up, to Jake's stepdad for all his help, and of course to the amazing Louisa Winter for letting us use this little piece of history. So, I hope you've all been practising at home, because we have a lot to get through!'

He nods at Lee who lets rip with his trumpet intro and the rest of us try to remember our cues and crash in and out clumsily until Marley waves his arms and stops us, and we take it from the top again. And again, and

193

again, with directions from Marley and a few tweaks from the rest of us, until 'Back Then' is sounding good once more.

It takes a while, but Sasha has clearly been practising because the vocals are really tight now, and we do sound more like a band and less like a rowdy class of Year Sevens messing about with the instruments when the music teacher nips out of the room.

Next, Marley, Dylan, Bex and Sasha run through the library song a few times. This has been put together jigsaw style, with the help of GarageBand links flying back and forth, but although it's basic it's sounding strong. Most of us have ideas about what our contributions might be, and two hours in we manage to have both songs sounding good. Marley calls another all-band practice for Wednesday.

'We have to step it up,' he says. 'This festival for the libraries is a real game changer. We've got the chance to support one of the best-loved stars of the sixties – Ked Wilder is a music industry giant. He knows everyone there is to know in the business, and if he likes the Lost & Found – well, I don't need to tell you what that means. It could be our ticket to fame and fortune!'

 194

Bex pulls a face. 'This whole festival is a marketing opportunity for you, am I right? I mean, I care about the band, obviously, but this festival is all about saving the libraries – that's what matters!'

'Definitely,' Marley agrees, staring Bex down with his trademark blue-eyed charm. 'And we can do that better if we're really well practised and our songs are the best they can be. So, I need to know if everyone's on board here. We'll have all-band practices on Mondays, Wednesdays and Fridays, and in between there'll be smaller, more focused meet-ups so we can work on whatever needs the most attention. If anyone thinks they'll struggle to do all this, tell me now – I'd rather know. I want everyone at practices; everyone – unless you've broken both legs or you're dying of some contagious tropical disease, be here, and be here on time. The more we put in, the more we get out – the stakes are high, for the libraries and for us as a band. Understood?'

There's a general murmur of agreement. Nobody says they can't manage the timetable, though not everyone looks overjoyed about it.

'What about you, Soumia?' Bex checks. 'You're in Year Eleven – haven't you got GCSEs at the moment? Are you sure you can fit in three practices a week alongside the revison? Are your parents going to be OK with it?'

Soumia shrugs. 'I'll make it work,' she says. 'I won't let you down.'

I frown. The idea of the Lost & Found was supposed to be a place to go to connect with others, not just one more chore in an already stressful teenage life.

'Be careful, Marley,' I tell him as I wash the hot chocolate mugs afterwards. 'I know how much you love this band, but don't push people too far – not everyone can be as committed as you are.'

'Why not?' he asks, genuinely puzzled. 'This is our big chance, don't you see? We've got an amazing sound and we're writing our own songs. And we're young – still at school – which gives us a unique selling point once the press get hold of it. If the world could just see what we're capable of, we'd go right to the top! You have to have vision. That's what Ked Wilder says in his book . . .'

'I knew I would live to regret getting you a library card,' I tease.

'You don't mean that,' he says, switching off the lights and locking the door as we make our way down the steps.

 196

'C'mon, I'll walk you home. I'm only pushing them because I care – you know that, don't you? We've got something special, Lexie. You know it, I know it – we'd be crazy not to run with it!'

Something special.

I sigh because I know without a doubt that Marley isn't talking about me and him. He's talking about the Lost & Found.

We're in the middle of Wednesday's practice, a particularly rowdy one where we're struggling to agree on how to arrange the harmonies for 'Going Places', when there's a sharp knock on the window. Louisa Winter appears in the doorway, striking as always in a paint-stained pinafore dress and a green silk bandana tied round her hair. The trademark paintbrushes are speared through her auburn waves, of course.

'Were we too noisy?' I say anxiously. 'I'm so sorry if the sound carried. We're working on a new song and it's still a bit chaotic . . .'

'The music is glorious,' she declares. 'But not loud enough to be heard up at the house. No, I'm sorry to disturb you, but I've just had a telephone call from your Miss Walker. Exciting news! The local TV news want to do a feature on the libraries, and they want to talk to me – and you! Reclusive lady artist and up-and-coming teen pop band . . . how about that?'

Marley jumps to attention. 'The TV?' he checks. 'Really? How soon? Because we'd planned to keep our set list for the festival under wraps for just a little while longer.'

Under wraps? This is Marley-speak for 'we only have three songs, we're seriously rough around the edges and I don't think we're ready for world domination until next week at the earliest'.

'They'll film it on Saturday to broadcast Tuesday,' Louisa is saying. 'I don't think they need a whole song – just a clip of a few of you playing in the library perhaps? And they want to talk to you, especially you, Lexie, and Marley – you spoke very well on the radio last weekend, it seems. Miss Walker is keen for Bex to be there, and then whoever else you want to bring along – possibly not the whole band. There are rather a lot of you! Miss Walker said six would be plenty . . .'

'Didn't I say we'd be famous?' Marley crows. 'I knew it! Didn't I tell you?'

Miss Winter just laughs. 'Fame is somewhat overrated,' she tells us. 'But it's not always easy to convince the young of that fact, especially these days. We're all a bit obsessed, it seems. Everybody can be famous for fifteen minutes, as Andy used to say. He had some very strange ideas on a lot of things, but with that one I have to admit he was spot on . . .'

'Who's Andy?' I whisper to Bex.

'Andy Warhol,' she whispers back. 'Super-famous pop artist. Bit of a weirdo. Friend of Miss Winter, clearly . . .'

'So the TV crew will be at Bridge Street Library at five o'clock on Saturday,' Louisa Winter tells us. 'Be there on time, and bring your instruments in case they do want an action shot of some kind. Oh, and I love what you've done with the place. Groovy, as we used to say back in the day! See you Saturday!'

Louisa Winter exits as dramatically as she arrived, leaving us in stunned silence. Thanks to the library campaign, we've already been on the radio and now a TV appearance is looming. This is great for the band, obviously. But, for me, perhaps it could be life-changing. Not everybody listens to the radio . . . but the TV? That's still pretty popular, right?

Anybody could be watching.

Even my mum. She might switch on the telly and catch a glimpse of the girl she left behind more than three years ago; she'd drop everything, of course, and call the TV station to track me down, and we'd be back together again. There are just those old niggles: why she'd need to spot me on TV in the first place, why she hasn't been to the police or social services trying to track me down and why she didn't come back in the first place. Amnesia, perhaps? If she's lost her memory, could a TV appearance trigger its return? I don't know.

'Lexie? You're crying,' Bex whispers, and I wipe away tears with my sleeve because I do not want to fall apart here, or now, or ever.

'One more time!' Marley calls out, oblivious to my meltdown, and the Lost & Found crash into action again.

Dear Mum,

Look out for me on Tuesday on the local news programme. I'm going to be talking about libraries and about the band I told you about. If you see it, I hope you recognize me – my hair's a bit different now, but I still look kind of the same.

I hate to write this, Mum, but I can't help wondering why you never came back. I felt bad for ages because you told me to stay where I was, but I couldn't. I had to move when the social services came, obviously. I've blamed myself for years. If I'd managed to stay at the flat, would you have come back? I don't know. I used to worry that you'd see me with Mandy and Jon, get angry that I was in a new family . . . so I've kept them at arm's length for all this time, and that wasn't fair. They've been so good to me, but I've always put you first, worried about what you might think. The truth is that you could still have found me easily, if you'd only come looking.

I don't think you did.

Love,
Lexie x

PS I'm going to put this letter in the
woodburner because it's not the kind of thing
I'd want you to see . . . if you actually could
see it, that is.

22

Something Special

'Mum?' I reach up to tug at the duvet, trying to wake her, but she just grunts and turns over, pulling the pillow over her head.

'Mum, wake up, please!' I say. 'I'm hungry, and there's nothing in the biscuit tin, and I've missed school again. I might be in trouble . . . we had tests today!'

Silence. The curtains are pulled shut against the sunshine and the room smells stale, stifling. Mum has been in bed for three days now. If I try to snuggle in with her, she pushes me away, and in the night I can hear her crying. She hasn't been taking her tablets.

'Mum?' I whimper.

She struggles into a sitting position. 'Get out of here, Lexie!' she growls. 'Give me some peace for once, please!'

I wake up crying, my eyes gritty with tears.

The nightmares are back.

On Tuesday at six o'clock, Bex and I are squashed on the sofa waiting for our small-screen debut; Mandy has her feet up on the coffee table, Jon is in the kitchen making popcorn and Mary Shelley is sitting on my knee, nibbling apple slices and blinking at the TV. Just to add to the fun, my mobile is bleeping every few seconds with messages from the rest of the Lost & Found guys.

Here we go! Happi texts. I hope Mum and Dad like the interview!

OMG! Sasha texts. They just mentioned us in the intro! I wonder what time our segment will be on?

Wish you were here, Marley texts. The suspense is killing me. I hope they cut that bit where they tried to talk to Sami and he just ignored them because he can't speak much English yet. Or maybe he's just rude, who knows? And the bit where you said we were all misfits. Not cool, Lexie, not cool.

Hurt, I stuff my mobile down the side of the sofa.

'What's up?' Bex asks. 'Trouble in paradise? Mr Wonderful being an idiot again?'

'Of course not,' I lie. 'I just don't want to be interrupted,

204

that's all. This waiting is making me nervous! I wish I hadn't said that thing about us all being misfits . . .'

'Why?' Bex says. 'It's true, isn't it?'

'I know, but what if it offends someone? Like Happi's parents, or Sami's aunt and uncle, or Romy's mum, or . . . well, anybody!'

'You didn't say it in a nasty way,' Bex says.

'You'll be brilliant,' Mandy adds firmly. 'Stop worrying.'

I do worry, though. We are a long way from brilliant. We've notched up another two practices, and the three songs are sounding strong – but they're still just three songs, and that's not enough for a festival set. Marley has stuck a calendar up inside the railway carriage and is crossing off the days until we play. When he's stressed, he gets snarky and gets on everyone's nerves.

'Popcorn coming up!' Jon calls through from the kitchen. 'D'you want butter and salt or a drizzle of honey?'

'Honey,' Bex calls back. 'Always!'

Jon passes the hot, sweet popcorn around. My mobile buzzes endlessly from underneath the cushions, and I ignore it, stroking Mary Shelley. And then, finally, the presenters start talking about the library closures, and the cameras cut away from the studio to Bridge Street Library.

Almost two hours of planning and filming has been cut down to just four minutes, but they are four awesome minutes all the same.

The film opens with a shot of the Lost & Found playing. We were told to bring just half the band, and there were a few disagreements over the line-up. Soumia pulled out at the last minute because her parents didn't want her to be on the telly, so Marley dragged in Sami instead. The silent, sad-eyed refugee kid has cheekbones like razor blades, the longest lashes I've ever seen on a boy and the kind of messy, wavy hair you want to run your fingers through.

In theory, obviously. Not in practice.

Anyway.

Marley said he was trying to get a balance of sound, but I noticed that he also picked the best-looking kids in the band to accompany us. Romy, shy and overweight, and George, with his glasses and acne-pitted skin, didn't make the shortlist.

It ended up being Marley, me, Bex, Sasha, Sami and

 206

Happi, with Jake lurking in the background as runner/manager/photographer.

The camera crew arranged us cleverly, sitting on tables, standing against bookshelves, Sasha sitting on a pile of books and peeking over a copy of *Harry Potter and the Philosopher's Stone* to sing the chorus from 'Back Then'.

It looks stunning. The camera layers in a hazy shot of Marley leaning in towards me as I do tambourine and backing vocals, adding an improvised harmony of his own. As that shot fades, we see Sami playing mournful flute on the book stacks behind Sasha, then a shot of Bex strumming bass guitar and Happi playing violin while sitting precariously on a half-height shelf.

It's short, but it's as perfect a snapshot as I have ever seen. Even without the frantic buzzing of my buried mobile, I know that Marley will be ecstatic – and Miss Walker too. They've managed to showcase not just the band but the library as well, and made both look seriously cool. As the camera cuts away to Miss Walker (in her library dress, naturally) telling the presenter that libraries are not just about books, I know that even the most stubborn and couldn't-care-less viewer will be sitting up a little straighter, keen to know more about this place where the librarian has hair the colour of candyfloss and teenagers drape themselves across the furniture to play songs they've written themselves.

I'm grinning as I watch Bex talking to camera, telling the whole of the Midlands that libraries belong to everybody. Marley is next, stretching the facts a little as he tells the camera that books inspired him to be a musician, and how the band is struggling now that we can't practise in the library any more.

'Doesn't let the truth stand in the way of a good story, our Marley,' Bex says scathingly.

'He sounds convincing, though,' Mandy says kindly. 'Seems like a nice boy!'

Bex just snorts, and then it's my turn to cringe as I'm on screen. To my relief they haven't used the bit about us being a bunch of misfits – it's all about how libraries have been a lifeline to me all through my childhood, and then a plea to the viewers for anyone who cares about libraries to write a letter to Millford Council asking them to stop the closures.

'Yessss!' Bex says, punching a fist into the air as Mandy and Jon whoop and cheer. 'Excellent!'

The film closes with a short interview with Louisa Winter, striking in a teal-blue velvet dress with her hair actually combed and swept into an updo without the help of paintbrushes. She is poised and confident and effortlessly clever, explaining why Millford Council should be celebrating culture, learning and creativity instead of starving it to death with endless cuts and closures. She tells viewers that her good friend, the legendary Ked Wilder, is so incensed at the threat to the library he loved so much, that he is coming to Millford to play a free concert in the park to protest about the closures.

'Ably supported by Millford's very own teen sensations, the Lost & Found!' Louisa Winter concludes, and the little film cuts back briefly to our library session before fading out to the studio.

'That is going to make a lot of people sit up and think,' Jon says, passing the popcorn round again. 'It was really persuasive. I get the feeling those TV people liked you!'

'Having Louisa Winter on your side is a bit of a coup too,' Mandy adds. 'She's a sweetheart, but fierce when she wants to be. And getting Ked Wilder involved – a stroke of genius!'

209

Jon grins. 'It's not just good news for the library, though. This band you're in, the Lost & Found. It's amazing! What a sound! A pity it was only half a minute's worth of music . . . that song was powerful!'

I take a soft breath in. Is it possible that out there somewhere my mum was watching? Would she recognize me, know that the song was about the two of us? Probably not.

'Bet a lot of parents watching that will be more supportive about the practices now,' Bex muses. 'Now they can see just what we're doing and why it matters. It should help Happi and Romy and Soumia. Maybe Sami too?'

'Maybe,' I say.

I rescue the buried mobile, ignoring a dozen messages from Marley, and call Happi and then Sasha to go over it all again, tell them how brilliant they were, how exciting it is to feel we're actually doing something positive for the library. I'm just about to call Romy to see what she thought of it when the doorbell rings.

I hear voices, and the next thing I know Marley Hayes is right there in our living room, guitar slung over his shoulder, accepting compliments on his TV appearance from Mandy and Jon and helping himself to popcorn.

210

'Come to play to us in person?' Jon teases, nudging the guitar, and Marley just laughs and says he takes it everywhere with him.

'You weren't answering your phone,' he says. 'So I thought I'd come over!'

'Oh, I . . . mislaid it,' I say, then realize it's right there in my hand, and Marley can see that. 'I just found it this minute. Sorry!'

'What's up, Marley?' Bex wants to know. 'Come to tell us how good we were? Or are you dragging everyone out for another practice?'

'Just calling for Lexie, really,' Marley says. 'I thought we could maybe go for a walk or something, or just hang out. But sure, you were good, Bex – everyone was. Amazing! That was the best piece of publicity ever – I bet we get mobbed in school tomorrow! I think we can say we've probably got a fan base now, and we haven't even played live yet.'

'Ugh,' Bex scowls. 'That's something to look forward to – getting mobbed by a bunch of Year Sevens. You are so shallow, Marley!'

'Bex!' Mandy warns. 'Enough! Marley's a guest in our house!'

Not for long, if I can help it.

'Walk then?' I prompt, tugging at his elbow. I promise Mandy and Jon I'll be back before dark and the two of us escape into the cool spring evening.

'It was pretty much perfect,' he is saying as we walk down towards the park. 'Shows what we can do when we try! Just wait till we get the whole of the band on TV – we'll blow 'em away!'

'It did look good,' I admit. 'I hope Romy and George didn't feel hurt that we didn't include them . . . not good for the confidence.'

'We were only allowed six people,' he reminds me. 'Makes sense to pick the ones that look good. Plus, we had a good balance sound-wise . . .'

'I guess. They cut the bit where I mentioned misfits,' I say. 'I didn't mean it in a bad way, Marley. I love everyone in the band!'

'I know you do,' he tells me. 'I shouldn't have mentioned it – I was a bit stressed out before the broadcast, but I should have known they'd do a good job. You were wonderful!'

We head into the park and Marley takes my hands and

dances me around on the grass until I'm laughing, but there's an ache in my chest tonight and I can't stay smiling for long. Marley doesn't notice.

'It really worked, didn't it, the bit where I helped with the harmonies?' he's saying. 'Maybe I could sing on some of the others too? Just backing, obviously. We do need to think about style, though. We looked OK in the film because of the library setting and everything, but a bunch of people on stage all dressed in their own stuff is going to look messy. I mean, where does Romy get her clothes? They're out of the ark, and not in a cool, vintage way, either. And Sami, with that ridiculous coat that's practically falling apart at the seams. And George. I mean . . . does his gran knit those cardigans?'

'Does it matter?' I ask.

'Of course, if we want to get to the top; everything matters!'

Perhaps that's the problem. I don't care about getting to the top, or about Romy's charity-shop clothes or Sami's coat or George's cardies. I like my friends the way they are. What matters to me are things like finding my mum and turning words into music and saving Bridge Street Library, and whether the boy I'm supposed to be going out with is ever going to kiss me again.

We head for the bandstand and sit on the steps, like Louisa Winter did in the magazine photos I saw in that old magazine. I feel all mixed up inside, and I know that some of it's to do with Mum – the radio and TV interviews, along with writing that first song, have dragged up hopes and memories that might have been better left alone. Last night's bad dream is like a shard of glass inside me.

Some of the upset feelings are to do with Marley, though.

Who do you ask about boy trouble when you don't have a mum? Not Mandy, who clearly thinks Marley is the perfect gentleman. Not Bex, who thinks he's a savage. Not Happi, who still has crushes on movie stars and thinks that thirteen is too young to have a boyfriend. Not Mary Shelley, who just looks at me with silent disdain whenever I try to tell her about Marley. I don't think she approves.

What would Mum say? That boys aren't worth it? That he's just being ultra polite and taking things slow? That this is the twenty-first century, and a girl needs to take things into her own hands? Maybe.

214

I shuffle up a little closer to Marley and lean against him casually as if I'm cold.

'This would be a great location for a proper music video,' he is saying. 'After the festival, maybe Ked Wilder will help us to find a record company and we can release a CD and make a video and get properly famous. There's nothing we can't do, Lexie, you and me, if we want it badly enough. We make a great team!'

'Is that what we are?' I whisper. 'A great team? Good friends? Songwriting partners?'

'All of that,' he says, and as if he's finally getting the message, his arm snakes round my waist and his head dips down so we're sitting cheek to cheek. 'You're cool, Lexie Lawlor. I've never met a girl like you – you're not just clever and creative and kind, you're determined as well. You're too good for me, I know that, but I honestly think that together we could take on the world . . .'

We sit for a moment in silence, and for that moment I think everything is going to be all right. Marley's cheek is warm against mine, his arm is wrapped round my waist. The park is so quiet this evening that I can almost hear his breathing, smell the faint aroma of popcorn on his breath.

215

I turn my face a little so that my nose nudges his . . . and then the moment is over.

Marley jumps up, unzips his gig case and takes out the guitar.

'I almost forgot,' he says, oblivious to the flare of shame in my cheeks. 'I've written the start of another song – I wanted you to hear it, get some feedback before I take it any further!'

He starts to play, fingers picking out an intricate and haunting melody, and I sit quietly and listen, tears stinging my eyes. It's a sad, lonely song, and that's exactly how I feel.

Dear Mum,

Things are moving very slowly with the cool boy.
I can't tell if he likes me or not. I've tried
making the first move myself, but I'm not very
good at it and it makes me feel shy. I don't
think he's shy, though. It's confusing.

I feel awful – like our one and only kiss put
him off for life. Maybe I should change my
toothpaste, or start wearing strawberry lip gloss, or
chew gum or something? I just can't work him
out at all, and sometimes I think maybe I don't
want to, so things aren't looking too hopeful
right now.

The Lost & Found did that song I wrote for
you on TV, and I talked to the camera, close up,
but I don't suppose you saw.

The nightmares are back, and I really don't
want to remember those things. It wasn't always
like that. We were happy sometimes, weren't we?

Love,
Lexie x

PS I am going to fold this letter into the shape
of a paper boat and push it out on to the lake. If
you're walking past, maybe it will catch your eye?

23

Library Love

The next day at school, as predicted, everyone is talking about the Lost & Found and our brief appearance on TV. As if by magic, posters have appeared around the school, A5 flyers featuring a photo taken during the library filming. There are only half of us in the picture, of course, but we look confident, cool – slightly mysterious. 'The Lost & Found', the poster announces. 'See them live with pop superstar Ked Wilder at the Libraries Festival in Millford Park on Saturday 10th June'.

'This'll be Jake's doing,' Happi says. 'He took a ton of pictures on his phone when we were filming. I reckon he's planned this; got the posters ready and put them up on the day after the film went live!'

'He's good,' I agree. 'Not sure if we need a tech guy just yet, and it's hard to manage a band with someone like Marley in it because he's totally a law unto himself, but Jake is great at publicity and making things happen! He found us the old railway carriage, he put us together with Louisa Winter and he's amazing with posters and flyers and stuff.'

'I'm calling a library campaign meeting for six o'clock tomorrow at the railway carriage,' Bex says. 'We need Jake for that; he's full of good ideas. I'll tell the others at band practice later.'

A swarm of Year Sevens come shoving their way along the corridor, falling into goggle-eyed silence as they catch sight of us. It's slightly surreal.

'Hey,' Happi whispers as the sea of Year Sevens parts politely to let us through. 'What is this? I don't like it!'

'Get used to it, girl,' Bex says. 'This is fame. It's happening; it's real. One TV show and a few posters and just look at those kids . . . they're staring at us like we come from another planet!'

219

'They always stare at you that way,' I point out truthfully, and she elbows me in the ribs.

Everyone turns up to Thursday's Save the Libraries meeting except, predictably, Marley and Dylan.

'What is it with Marley Hayes?' Bex wants to know. 'He expects us to jump through hoops for his band – I swear, my fingers are practically raw after last night's practice – but he can't show up for this, even though it's the very thing that has given us our first festival slot! Idiot!'

I don't correct her, but I'm sad. Marley had said he'd be here, and Bex is right, the festival is a big deal for the band. The least he could do is be here to find out what's being planned. As Happi hands round juice and cookies and the others settle on the ancient bench sofas, Bex consults her notebook.

'OK. Jake, what's the latest on the festival?'

Jake takes over, reminding everyone of the festival date and explaining that Louisa Winter and the adult campaigners are sorting this particular part of the protest.

'Miss Winter is friends with the family who run Glastonbury, I think,' he explains. 'She'll have all the right

220

contacts and make sure it's cool, even if it's on a smaller scale. The council gave permission for a half-day festival event before the newspaper announced it was going to be all about the libraries, and now they can't go back on it – irony, much? Anyway, we'll have a stage in the park, some chill-out tents, and local food and trade stalls. Ked Wilder is playing at half two, so the only bit we need to worry about is being ready for our half-hour set beforehand . . .'

'Half an hour?' George echoes. 'No way! How many songs do we need to fill that?'

'Six or seven, Marley reckons,' Jake says. 'Five, minimum. With a bit of patter in between to spin things out. At the moment we've got three, but Marley and Lexie are working on it. It's got to be doable, right?'

There is some debate about this, but everybody's willing to try their best, and after a while Bex pulls us back to the point again, updating us on the letters campaign, the petition, the push to get primary-school kids to sign up for a library card.

'Finally . . . Louisa Winter is doing a piece in the *Gazette* this weekend, possibly with Lexie here too, because the paper loves the whole angle of teens taking action and the letters idea was hers originally, as you all know. Let's get a buzz going, let the council know just how many people care.'

Bex thanks everyone for coming along to the meeting and things relax a bit, with people asking questions or forming little groups to plan what they'll be doing. One by one, people start to leave, and I put the kettle on for warm water to wash up while I collect stray mugs to rinse at the sink. When I go back to the sink the window is all steamed up. I reach out a finger and trace something quickly before the steam clears.

When Sami moves towards me, I step aside automatically to let him pass, but instead he touches my arm.

'Letter?' he says, pushing a fold of paper into my hands.

I unfold the paper and there is a perfect library love letter: a heartfelt note telling the council what Bridge Street Library means to him as a young refugee struggling to settle down in Millford, thousands of miles from home. I'm amazed that he has been able to write so clearly and with such feeling.

'It is good?' he asks quietly. 'The letter? It will help your fight, Lexie?' My eyes widen because I don't think I have

222

heard him say more than a couple of words before. I assumed his English was poor, that he didn't understand much of what was being said around him, but it looks like his silence is from choice, not necessity.

'It's perfect,' I tell him, and his face breaks into a grin that somehow lifts my spirits too. 'Thank you, Sami – can I photocopy it? Show it to the newspaper?'

'Of course,' he says. 'I am happy to help. I am happy to make you smile.'

And he walks away, a tall, skinny boy with hair like a bird's nest, in a coat that really is as dodgy as Marley said: grubby and worn and frayed at the seams, and way too warm for a sunny May evening.

I'm still smiling.

24

Train of Thought

Bex, Jake, Happi and I end up making fruit smoothies and hanging out until the light fades. The old railway carriage feels like our space, a neutral territory where we can relax, be ourselves. Mostly, we're just chatting and chilling, but Jake is also mapping out rough designs for his new Love Letters flyer, Bex is making a new list of who has promised to do what, Happi is checking the library social media pages and I am trying not to get cross about the text that's just buzzed in from Marley.

> Sorry for the no-show.
> Something came up.

'Marley Hayes is driving me nuts,' I say, reading the text again and failing to spot any sign of an explanation. 'He's just texted me to apologize for not turning up, though he doesn't sound especially sorry. '*Something came up*, he says. What does that even mean?'

'Maybe he got sidetracked writing a song?' Jake suggests.

'Maybe it was a family thing?' Happi offers.

'Maybe it was a girl,' Bex states, and I feel tears stinging my eyes and blink them away before anyone can see.

'C'mon, Bex,' Jake cuts in. 'I know you don't like him, but don't blacken his name when he's not here to defend himself . . .'

'Whatever,' Bex snaps. 'I don't like him because I don't want Lexie to get hurt. I've never seen him with anyone for more than two weeks. He'd be better off getting a job at Millford tip than trying for the music business because dumping is his number-one skill. We've seen how he takes you for granted, Lexie. I just worry – that's all!'

'I'm fine!' I argue. 'We're OK, honest!'

'That's not what you said a minute ago,' Happi points out gently.

'Well, no, but that's because the text bugged me,' I say. 'In general, most of the time, I'm OK.'

'Are you?' Bex questions. 'I'm not so sure. I've seen it before, Lexie, remember? The feeling low, feeling sad. The whole point of this Lost & Found thing was to make new friends, have more fun, and I'm enjoying it, but I'm not so sure about you!'

Bex is right – I'm sad, missing Mum, feeling lost all over again.

Missing. What does that word even mean? A person vanishes and the person left behind misses them. Who is missing, really? Mum or me? Who is really lost?

I can't ask my friends about this, explain how anxious I feel every time I have to do or say something that might end up on the radio or TV, or in the *Millford Gazette*. Bex would tell Mandy, and she'd tell Josie my social worker, and I'd end up back in counselling with a well-meaning therapist asking me to act out my feelings with rag dolls or drawings or lumps of play dough. No thank you.

'It had better not be Marley Hayes making you sad,' my foster sister declares. 'I'll kill him!'

227

'That probably wouldn't help,' Jake tells her. 'If things are a bit up and down with Marley, you just need to talk it through. I'm not really an expert, but isn't that what they always say?'

'None of us are experts,' Bex concedes. 'But we do care about you!'

'Is he too pushy?' Happi wants to know. 'Boys like Marley can be. Stick to holding hands . . . these things can escalate. I've been reading about it in one of my church pamphlets!'

'Church pamphlets?' Jake checks. 'You're kidding, right?'

'Deadly serious,' Happi insists. 'Better safe than sorry! Look at the figures for teenage pregnancy.'

'Excuse me!' I interrupt. 'Just so you know, that will not be an issue. Seriously. I can't work out how Marley feels about me, that's all. If he sees me as a friend, a girlfriend, a writing partner or something else completely. Maybe I'm not ready for this whole boyfriend/girlfriend thing.'

'Let's face it – it was never going to be easy,' Bex says. 'Having Marley Hayes as your first boyfriend is a bit like picking Tolstoy's *War and Peace* as your first reading book. Jake's right – talk to him, Lexie. Sort it out, or end it on good terms because if you two fall out then we're all in

228

trouble. The Lost & Found is stuffed if one of you leaves, and that can't happen. Not before the festival, anyway!'

'No pressure then,' I note, cracking a smile.

'Definitely no pressure,' Bex says, and winks.

I look towards the window by the kettle, but the steamed-up glass has long since cleared, and my message has gone.

The next day, Year Ten tough girl Sharleen Scott grabs me by the collar of my blazer as I'm putting some science books back in my locker in a deserted school corridor.

'Tell your boyfriend to back off,' she growls, her face so close to mine that I can smell stale cigarette smoke on her breath. 'He's an animal; flew at my Darrel last night and attacked him for no reason at all! Marley's just jealous because we're not together any more, and because I won't join your poxy band. He's been nagging me to get involved for weeks, but he won't get the message. I. Am. Not. Interested. Not in him, not in the band. Understand?'

I understand that she's crazy, possibly delusional, but I have the sense not to say this. She lets me go with one last

229

shove just as the bell rings for lunch and Jake and Happi come miraculously round the corner.

'Oi!' Jake yells, breaking into a run. 'What's going on?'

'Nothing that need concern you, Scruff Boy,' Sharleen sneers, swaggering away.

'What did she do?' Happi demands, straightening my blazer and giving me a hug. 'Are you OK?'

'I'm fine, honest,' I say, picking up my scattered books. 'Just a bit shocked – and confused. She reckons Marley attacked her boyfriend last night. She made out he's jealous because she's with someone else, and that he's been pestering her to join the band!'

'In her dreams,' Jake mutters. 'But she's right about one thing – Dylan just told me the reason they didn't show last night. Marley got in a fight on the way home from school. Again . . .'

A whole raft of emotions fizz through me: fear, anger, confusion, disappointment. I don't know what to think or how to feel. I take out my mobile, and there are six unread texts from Marley in the last hour telling me he needs to talk, needs to see me fast before Sharleen Scott starts shooting her mouth off.

230

Too late.

Where are you? I text back. **What happened?**

Meet me behind the gym, five minutes, he replies, and like an idiot I tell Jake and Happi not to stress and trudge off to find him.

The back of the gym is out of bounds. It's not difficult to spot the lone figure sitting beneath an oak tree beside the perimeter fence, reading the Ked Wilder library book. I almost turn back there and then because I can see his beautiful face is bruised and swollen, and I can't be sure whether I am sympathetic or furious.

'Lexie,' he calls. 'Over here!'

As I get closer, I see the blue-black bruises blooming on his right cheek, the split lower lip with its blister of dark, dried blood.

'Oh, Marley, what have you done?'

'I know, I know . . . I'm an idiot,' he says. 'I just walk into it, every single time. It's like I can't help it.'

I notice that a few slats of wood in the fence have worked loose, making a gap that a person could fit through.

'This is my escape route when school is bugging me,' he tells me. 'One side of the fence is rules and tests and snarky teachers, and the other side is freedom. Cool, right?'

'What will you do when they mend the gap in the fence?'

Marley grins. 'They've mended it twice already,' he argues. 'I just make sure it never stays mended for long . . .'

I sit down beside him, and it's quiet and peaceful after the madness of school, where too many kids push and shove their way though the day. Sunlight filters through the dappled leaves and somewhere in the distance birds are singing.

'About Sharleen,' I say. 'Too late. We had a chat . . .'

Marley swears under his breath. 'Whatever she said, it's probably lies,' he tells me. 'She's a spiteful little troublemaker; don't know what I ever saw in her. She's been hassling me for the last few weeks to put her in the band, and I've just laughed it off . . . Like I said, she's got a voice like a bag of rusty nails. Then, walking home from school last night me and Dylan bumped into her with her boyfriend. He's this big thug from St Michael's High: six foot tall, total bonehead. Not sure what she's been telling him about me, but he wasn't exactly friendly.'

 232

'Her story was a bit different,' I say. 'She reckons you've been nagging her to join the band, that you still fancy her . . .'

Marley snorts, outraged. 'That's rubbish! You know that,' he tells me. 'They were winding me up. He called me a load of stuff and Sharleen egged him on. You can't let that kind of thing go, can you?'

'You can, actually,' I say. 'You just hold your head up and walk past, and tell yourself you're better than all that. You should try it some time.'

Marley sighs. 'Maybe.'

I grit my teeth, exasperated. 'What is it with you, Marley? Your face is a mess! What if this had happened just before the festival? Our big chance? What if he'd stamped on your fingers or broken your wrist so you couldn't play guitar? Or actually kicked your guitar to splinters?'

'Dylan ran off with the guitar,' Marley says. 'Raised the alarm, found some lads who chased the kid away. It could have been worse.'

'You have to stop this,' I tell him. 'Seriously, you do. For my sake, if not your own. For the band's sake. Put the music first, the way you expect us to!'

233

Marley is silent, folorn. A part of me feels sorry for him, but a bigger part feels scared and daunted. Do I really know this boy at all? He keeps so much of himself hidden it's difficult to work out what's real and what isn't.

The fighting thing – it's scary, messed up.

'I'm trying,' he says eventually. 'For you, because I know it bugs you.'

'It doesn't bug me, Marley,' I say. 'That makes it sound trivial, and it isn't, OK? It matters. You have this reputation for being tough and stupid and never walking away from a fight. It's like you deliberately pick people who are bigger and harder than you too – you know you'll come off worst and you just don't care.

'One day you're going to get more than a few bruises and a fat lip – you'll get properly hurt! Do you like getting beaten up? Because I don't like it, Marley, I really, really don't!'

As I speak, Marley looks out into the distance, impassive. I can't tell if he's listening, if he understands or cares. And then he turns to me, and his blue eyes are damp with tears. My anger evaporates, like it was never there at all.

'Lexie, I'm sorry,' he says, and he puts his arms round me, holding me tight. 'You're right. I'll stop, I promise. I will. For you, and for the band.'

We hang on to each other forever maybe, or maybe it's just a few seconds. I press my lips softly against the bruises on his face, slide my fingers over his ruined mouth, wipe away the tears.

Somewhere in the distance, the bell rings to signal the end of lunch, but when I ask Marley if he's coming to lessons he just shakes his head, stands and slips quietly through the gap in the fence.

I walk back into school alone.

Train of Thought

Well, I'm riding on this train of thought
I wonder, where . . . where will I get off?
Will it be your eyes?
Will it be your smile?
Lost in my head now
For quite a while.

Been travelling on for many days
Oh but I'm starting to forget your ways.
Money's getting low.
Time ain't on my side.
Been jumping tracks
For a place to hide.

This old train shows no sign of slowing.
Just can't recall quite where I'm going.
No I can't deny
I'm feeling blue.
Cos more and more
Thoughts are not with you.

I'm riding on this train of thought
And I wonder, where . . . where will I get off?

25

Half-Term

'Is this song about us?' Marley wants to know the minute he's listened to the GarageBand link. 'If so, I think you should stay aboard the train. I'd miss you if you jumped.'

'I won't jump unless you push me,' I promise.

'Why would I do that?'

Too many reasons to mention, Marley. Way too many.

'The song's not about us, anyway,' I bluff. 'Just a story. The old railway carriage inspired it . . . I was thinking, playing with words.'

Fiction is definitely a skill of mine; the lies drip off my tongue like honey.

237

I save my truths, my secrets, for the lyrics of our songs . . .
nobody would ever spot them there, hiding in plain sight.

Marley checks another three practices off on the calendar,
and then somehow it's half-term. We have four songs now,
four songs that sound great on a good day in the railway
carriage, but Marley isn't satisfied.

He's still reading the Ked Wilder biography and tells us
that Wilder spent two years doing a gig a night in pubs and
clubs all over the UK to perfect his sound. He played his
set so many times, in so many places, that it became second
nature. Practice, Marley says, is the key to success, and even
though we are rehearsing three times a week it's not enough.

'We're a new band,' Marley tells us. 'Still raw and rough
around the edges, but we've been given a chance to get
noticed. Maybe it's too soon, maybe I'm crazy to think we
can do it, but we've got to give it our best shot, surely? We
have to try.'

'What are you saying, Marley?' Bex asks. 'Four practices
a week? Five?'

'Every day,' he says grimly. 'Afternoons are no good
because the treatment room has bookings, but if we get

238

here at nine, that's three good hours, plus the usual three evenings . . .'

'Too much, dude,' Dylan grumbles. 'It's half-term. I need my lie-ins!'

'Fair enough,' Marley says. 'I've had offers from two other kids in the school who'd like to be our drummer if you drop out. Shall I get in touch?'

'You can't throw me out of the band!' Dylan snorts. 'For wanting a lie-in? For having a moan because you're swapping school with five days of extra practice?'

'Seven days,' Marley corrects him. 'Saturday and Sunday too.'

'You're havin' a laugh, big brother. I'll say it if they won't – too much.'

Marley rakes a hand through his fringe and scans the practice room, his blue eyes determined.

'I don't think you understand what we're doing here,' he says. 'What we've got. We have the best musical talent Millford Park has on offer, hand-picked – everything from classically trained musos like Happi, Romy and George to kids who've taken school music lessons and turned out to be amazing, like Soumia, Sasha, Bex and Lee, and

239

self-taught talents like Sami, who totally blows me away, and even my annoying little brother. Then there's me, a gobby pain with big dreams and slave-driver tendencies, but I can write music. Lexie here can pull lyrics out of thin air and wrap the music around them to bring it all alive, make magic. We need every one of you – even Jake, who might not play but holds us all together, sorts the techie stuff, takes the photos.

'There is nothing quite like us out there in the world, nothing as weird and wonderful and cool, nothing with such great vocals, such haunting string and brass and woodwind sections. In three weeks' time we have the chance to be seen and heard by thousands of people, to help the libraries, make a difference. And if we are good enough, maybe – just maybe – we will catch the eye of pop royalty Ked Wilder. Imagine if that happens – just imagine! It can't happen, though, unless each and every one of us pulls our weight. So if I seem like a slave-driver, well, I'm sorry. That's why.'

When Marley finishes speaking, he is greeted by whistles and cheers and one of Lee's euphoric trumpet blasts. I think that if the Lost & Found don't make it as a band,

Marley has a future in TV or film, or possibly politics, because he knows exactly how to get an audience in the palm of his hand.

Jake steps forward, awkward and uncertain after Marley, but equally passionate.

'I'm the one on the outside,' he tells us. 'I get to watch, to fix up the mics, check the sound, take the pictures. I see it from a distance, and Marley is right – there is something amazing going on here. So what if we lose a few lie-ins? So what if we have to actually work for this? It will be worth it just to know we tried our very best. I think we'd be mad to give up now!'

Looking around, I can see the fire in Marley's eyes reflected in us all, even Dylan. We're willing to go the extra mile, give it everything, because what he and Jake have said is true. The Lost & Found has something special, something amazing, and we'd be crazy not to push that as far as it can go.

Astonishingly, Lee is the only one of all of us to be away on holiday for the half-term week, and Jake promises to send him daily GarageBand links so he can keep up with where we're at.

'Take your trumpet,' Marley instructs. 'Play every day. Maybe a bit of Cornish sun will add something new to the mix!'

The rest of us turn up obediently every morning at nine. On the first day, Bex jokes around, pretending to take the register, but we all know that Marley is keeping tabs on us anyway, and that for him it's not a joke. Three days in, he talks to Romy about her timekeeping; she arrives late every day. Remembering his past comments about Romy's weight and clothes, I'm terrified he'll say something harsh or hurtful, but the two of them wander off across the grass, talking quietly, and a few minutes later when I glance across they are hugging, Romy wiping her eyes.

'What happened?' I ask Marley later, in the Leaping Llama. 'Is she going to turn up on time from now on?'

'Hopefully,' he tells me. 'But if she can't, we'll manage. Special circumstances. Never let it be said that I'm some kind of tyrant!'

'What special circumstances?' I ask. Romy joins us for lunch at school every day, and I see her as a friend now, but she's still quite shy and guarded. I'm surprised she's confided in Marley.

 242

'She'll tell you herself when she's ready,' he explains. 'But basically Romy's mum is ill and her dad's not around, so she's left to do most of the caring. This week, the two of them are struggling. I said a late start was OK as long as she was willing to put in the work once she gets here . . .'

He gets another hug for that, from me. Underneath the tough exterior, Marley Hayes has a kind heart. I think he cares about the Lost & Found in ways that aren't just to do with music.

'We're all a bit messed up,' he says. 'One way or another. I know a little bit of Romy's story, and the basics of Happi's and Sami's. I know that you and Bex are in foster and there'll be stories behind that, and you'll tell me one day maybe, or maybe not. We all have stuff we keep hidden. You called us a band of misfits, and you were right – there's probably not a single one of us who's actually normal. Whatever normal is . . .'

'It's normal to be a bit messed up,' I say. 'Nobody's perfect. Except Sasha perhaps, and Soumia, but even then I'm not so sure. So what? It's OK.'

Marley laughs. 'I'll tell you something, Lexie. It's not just OK – it's our secret weapon. We've all been through

243

something. We all know what it's like to hurt, to feel lost and misunderstood. And we're not afraid to take that feeling and feed it into the music. That's where it comes from, the magic – from the things we hide away, the secrets, the sadness. That's what I think, anyway!'

I think that Marley Hayes has the soul of a poet, that I will never meet any boy I like so much in the whole world. Then he spoils it all by telling me that Romy looks a mess, that I should have a word with her about her clothes and her weight.

'I don't have a problem with Romy's weight!' I argue. 'You're the only one who's bothered about that – do your own dirty work!'

'Two weeks and four days,' he tells me. 'Less than three weeks, and we have to stand up on a stage in front of thousands of people. Even before we open our mouths, they'll be judging us. You know that, Lexie!'

'Yes, but they'll be there to see Ked Wilder, not us,' I point out. 'Or if they are there for us, then it'll just be from curiosity, because of what they've seen in the papers and stuff. They're not going to be judging us on appearances!'

244

'You think?' he challenges me. 'How else do we make our first impressions on the world around us? We need a look, Lexie. Something basic, simple, to pull the band together visually. Ked Wilder put his backing band in black drainpipe jeans and turtlenecks and winklepicker boots . . .'

'I am not wearing those horrible pointy boots!' I grumble. 'Or black jeans. Black leggings, maybe, and a skirt and T-shirt . . . What if we just have black as a theme? Maybe with a few bits of red to brighten it up a bit? Have Sasha in a red dress at the front?'

Marley grins. 'Might work,' he says. 'Yeah, we'll try it! I'll tell the others tomorrow, get them to wear black and red for the next day's practice. Once this week is up, we'll be on a real countdown. Time's going to fly past. We need to be ready. And we still need one more song . . .'

'Anything in the pipeline?' I ask.

'I'm working on a few things, but they're not quite right,' he tells me. 'Every time I think I've struck gold, it turns out to be a riff I've stolen from some other song without realizing it. I'll keep trying.'

'I'll keep trying too, I promise.'

*

At the end of the week, we have our first internet sensation, and it's library linked, not Lost & Found. Happi has posted a screenshot of Sami's Library Love Letter online, and suddenly it's going viral on Twitter and Facebook, with hundreds of shares and thousands of likes.

Sami looks baffled by it all, but when Miss Walker rings Bex from the library to tell us a national newspaper has seen the post and would like to speak to Sami, everything goes crazy. The *Daily News* have a freelance reporter and photographer in the area who can be at Bridge Street Library within the hour, if Sami can be there.

'Will you do it?' Bex pleads.

Sami looks from Bex to Happi to me and back to Bex again, and then he shrugs and says he'll try. Marley, forced to wind up the morning practice half an hour early, takes charge of Sami, coaching him to mention the festival and namecheck the Lost & Found. He tries to coax Sami out of the ancient, threadbare overcoat he wears everywhere, but Sami won't budge on that.

We walk him down to Bridge Street Library, me and Marley and Bex and Jake and Happi, and Miss Walker meets us, so excited she's practically fizzing, her candy-pink bouffant updo bobbing as she rushes about making everything look perfect. She shows us her latest display – a wall of letters from authors, illustrators, musicians, artists, actors and assorted other famous names, all mixed in with school kids, pensioners and locals; Sami's letter is somewhere in the middle.

'We've sent copies of every letter to the council,' Miss Walker explains. 'And lots of people will have sent their letters straight there, of course. But I couldn't resist putting these ones up. It cheers me up just to see how much people care!'

It's a bright, joyful patchwork of library love, and the photographer ends up standing Sami against it, his dark eyes staring out from under a mess of bird's-nest hair. His coat hangs loose and his arms cradle half a dozen books as if they're some kind of treasure.

When the reporter steps in to talk to Sami, I wonder if he will speak at all, let alone parrot back the speech Marley mapped out for him. Asked why he cares so much about Bridge Street Library, he is silent for so long that the reporter repeats the question, then looks around as if to check whether Sami speaks English after all.

247

'When I came here to England, I knew nothing,' he says abruptly, his voice calm and clear. 'This library taught me everything, took me in, gave me a safe place to be. This library saved my life.'

The reporter switches her recorder off, grinning.

'Perfect,' she says.

The next day, Sami's photo is on page five of the *Daily News*, along with a full transcript of his letter, under the headline 'Refugee Boy Speaks Up for the Library that Saved Him'.

Everyone agrees that it is indeed pretty much perfect.

Dear Mum,

I have never worked so hard in my life. There are just ten days until the protest festival and even though school has started again, we're practising almost every day. I've sung those songs so much I hear them in my dreams, or in my nightmares, rather. I am supposed to be writing another song, but I can't . . . I'm stuck.

School is busy too – we've set up this thing called Library Squad where we go into primary schools and talk to the kids and encourage them to sign up for a library card and write a Library Love Letter. We've been to five schools, and in four of those the teachers have marched the kids along to the Bridge Street Library to get their very own golden ticket. Miss Walker says membership numbers have never been higher, and that if it gets much crazier the computers might crash from the strain of it all.

I don't think things are working with the boy I was telling you about. No kisses, just the occasional hug and a kiss on the nose now and then, as if I am five years old. He is a very complicated boy. I know he's ambitious and mad about music. He has a way of carrying the rest of us along with that, so we believe in it too, and we're willing to jump through hoops to please him. There is a darker side to him, though. I just can't work it out, and that scares me a bit.

I miss you, Mum. I'm having nightmares again about the bad times. I wonder if I'll ever get over losing you.

Love,

Lexie x

PS I'm going to press send, even though this is a made-up email address. You never know.

Send

26

Time Flies

She throws a suitcase on to the bed, opens the wardrobe and flings an armful of bright clothes into it. 'Come on, Lexie!' she exclaims. 'Let's go – we don't belong here! I was thinking Cornwall, or north Wales . . . what d'you reckon?'

'Not yet,' I plead. 'It's the school trip next week. It's going to be cool! We could go after that maybe? If you still want to?'

Mum's face darkens, and fear seeps through my body like a virus. I have seen this before, seen how quickly Mum can flip from elated to angry to totally wiped out. I used to be able to calm her with a hug, a promise, but the older I get the harder it's becoming.

'Of course I'll still want to go,' she says, sulkily. 'Where's your sense of adventure, Lexie? You're no fun any more. So boring!'

'Mum, have you been taking your tablets? You don't seem yourself just now. You should see the doctor . . .'

'Don't tell me what I should and shouldn't do!' she rages, and her hand flies up as if to lash out . . .

The bedroom light snaps on, and I sit up, blinking. Mandy is in the doorway, her face creased with sleep and worry.

'Are you OK?' she asks. 'You were calling out in your sleep . . .'

'I'm fine,' I mumble, although I'm really not. My heart is racing and my cheeks are wet with tears.

'Nightmare?' Mandy asks, sitting down on the edge of the bed. 'That hasn't happened in a while. Want to talk about it?'

I shake my head. Talking to Mandy about how my mum wasn't the perfect parent I've always made her out to be would feel like a betrayal. I am carrying enough guilt already. Sometimes I think the weight of it will crush me.

'Just a bad dream,' I whisper.

I've kept the bad memories buried for a while now – I thought they were gone for good, but no, here they are again, shoving their way into my dreams. It must be the stress of the festival gig and things with Marley that are dragging them back into the open, or maybe the soul-searching and songwriting.

What's the point of dwelling on the bad stuff? It just messes with your head and your heart.

'You can always tell me if you need to – you know that, don't you?' Mandy says softly. 'I'm on your side, always.'

'Thanks,' I whisper.

When she leans down to hug me, I try to hug her back, but, as usual, the guilt gets in the way and I lie there passive, like a rag doll, one hand uselessly patting Mandy's shoulder. She tucks me in, switches off the light and creeps away, and I roll over, turning my face to the wall.

It takes a while for the Lost & Found to sort out their stage costumes. You'd think that everyone had a few items of black clothing hanging about, but this is clearly not the case. A bunch of us go trawling the charity shops one day after school. Sasha discovers a scarlet prom dress with a sweetheart neckline and a red bandana for her hair. Happi finds a black beaded top and a black tulle ballerina skirt. Bex spots a black mesh top to wear over a red vest with black skinny jeans, and plans to dye her hair crimson especially for the gig. Me, I've already got a tunic top and leggings, so that leaves Romy.

We put her in a baggy black T-shirt with leggings, black mini, red socks and black Doc Marten boots, and she looks amazing – even Marley approves. We manage an early dress rehearsal with everyone in black and red, and for the first time ever we actually look like a band as well as sounding like one. Sasha acts as unofficial stylist, and she's good; she brings along a binbag of accessories found on our charity-shop trawl. Adding a hat here and a scarf there, she somehow manages to pull things together and still allow everyone to keep their own style and individuality.

'OK,' Marley declares, looking awesome himself in a red T-shirt and black skinny jeans. 'We have got this thing sorted, image-wise. Good work, Sasha, all of you! Oh, hang on – Sami, can you drop the coat? It's not the right image, y'know?'

'I like the coat,' Sami says.

'I know you like the coat,' Marley says patiently. 'We've all noticed that you like the coat. Fine, whatever. But we're trying for a unified look here, and seriously that coat does not fit.'

253

There's a kind of silent stand-off when Marley glares at Sami and Sami gazes back, sad-eyed but stubborn. I worry for a moment that Marley's going to react the way he did with Dylan and threaten to dump Sami from the band, because I am pretty sure Sami would walk away without a moment's hesitation. In the end, Marley just sighs and tells Sami he can't wear the coat on stage at the festival. The stare-out is over, but it's impossible to guess who's won. Interestingly, I don't think it's Marley.

'Photo shoot?' Jake asks coaxingly, and we all pile outside to mess around in front of the old railway carriage while he shoots image after image on his iPhone. When we check the pictures on the band's Instagram page, even I raise an eyebrow because we look good, with Lee playing his trumpet and Bex pulling faces and Dylan and George leaning together while Sami hides beneath a hat Sasha has given him, still in the big coat. I'm with Happi and Romy, striking a cheesy pose and waving my tambourine in the air, and only Soumia, Marley and Sasha actually look poised and sane. It looks great, though, as if we've just stepped offstage and relaxed for a moment, which is kind

of what we have done. Plus, the railway carriage makes the best backdrop ever.

Things are coming together; we can all sense it. We're sounding better, tighter than ever before; we're looking cool – and now, finally, we are feeling confident too. Well, most of us.

Marley is on a permanent high because he has written another melody at last and is nagging me daily to sort some lyrics for it. I try, but when I'm stressed and anxious the words don't come easily and everything's so hectic I can't find the time or the space to really focus. I try not to worry too much, but the pressure to come up with something sits on my shoulders like a rucksack full of bricks.

I tell myself that the feeling will pass, that the words will come.

Nine days before the festival, Bex gets an email from one of her favourite YA authors, Rae Kelly, saying that she'd be happy to come up from London to support the protest.

'Whoa,' Bex breathes. 'She says she's happy to do a book event at the festival, and she'll sign books and

255

speak on stage about the libraries – whatever we want her to do.'

'That's amazing! I think there's going to be a tent just for author events and workshops. I'm going to go along, if I get a chance.'

'It's going to be cool,' Bex declares. 'Miss Walker says there'll be a karaoke with book-themed songs, a children's book character fancy dress and a workshop where kids can put themselves into a story and then take it away to print out. The librarians are dressing up as famous book characters to do storytelling, and a friend of Miss Walker's is doing a workshop on making things like bunting and paper flowers out of old, damaged books . . .'

'I can't wait,' I say. 'The community groups are all doing stalls too – just raising awareness of everything a library does, really. And Louisa Winter says she's bringing a few big name friends along . . . It's going to be epic!'

The *Millford Gazette* seems to think so too. They have nailed their colours to the mast and come out as library supporters. They're giving us loads of great coverage too. They run a double-page spread all about the festival, mapping out what's going on: several local bands are playing, but we are astonished to find that we are the only one scheduled to play on the stage. The others, a couple of pub bands and some teen acts, including the delightful Sharleen Scott, will be playing in one of the tents – the Music Zone, as the *Gazette* calls it.

The Lost & Found will be up on the main stage, though, opening for Ked Wilder. Seeing that in black and white in the pages of a newspaper is a bit of a reality check.

Song, I think, fear of failure curdling in my belly again. I'm feeling quite low and lost, but I have to push through it, find some words. I have to turn Marley's music into a song. If I fail, we all fail. Four songs are not enough to make an opening set, and we are running out of time. *Don't think about it*, I tell myself. *Don't think about failing in public, letting everybody down. You can do this. Chill out, give yourself a chance.*

But still no words come.

'This festival has set the whole town buzzing,' Mandy comments. 'Everyone I know is planning to go, and people from outside Millford too. Jon's got friends from Yorkshire coming down specially, and my mum and her friends are travelling from Northampton. They used to be big Ked

Wilder fans, back in the sixties – just wait until they see you two with your band! They'll be so proud!'

Next, the *Millford Gazette* runs a copycat feature on Sami's letter. It causes quite a stir, and a few days later they come out to cover a Library Squad visit – me, Bex and Happi talking in a primary school assembly and walking the class down to Bridge Street so every child can get a library card. The photos capture the kids writing their Library Love Letters, decorating them with paint and glitter and feathers. The following day, there's a full colour page in the paper. There's a picture of me with a bunch of kids around me, and my stupid heart leaps with hope yet again in case, somehow, my mum sees that picture and finds me.

That doesn't happen, obviously.

'Are you OK, Lexie?' Bex asks one evening after band practice. 'You've gone all quiet on me again. Are you stressed because of trying to write that last lot of lyrics? I wouldn't blame you. Time's racing past . . .'

'Don't remind me!'

I'm helping Bex to dye her hair red, ready for the big day. She is wrapping her head in tin foil to stop the sludgy dye dripping while I mop up the spills and tidy the sink.

 258

Right now, it looks like a scene of carnage, the aftermath of a particularly gory stabbing. Mary Shelley stares at us from the laundry basket, eyes narrowed in what could be despair.

'Nothing else on your mind?' Bex checks.

Can I say to Bex the things I couldn't say to Mandy? Maybe. I could try.

Bex is not a replacement mum, after all – more of a big sister/bestie combo, someone I can rely on to tell it like it is.

I sigh. 'I'm just . . . thinking about Mum a lot, lately. Is that crazy? It's all this stuff in the papers and on the radio and TV. I keep wondering what would happen if she saw me, recognized me, remembered . . .'

Bex looks dismayed. 'Oh, Lexie, no . . . that must be awful,' she says. 'Like a kind of self-torture. You do know she'd have been in touch by now if she could, Lexie? Or . . . if she wanted to?'

The tears come from nowhere, sliding down my face like rain, and Bex puts her arms round me awkwardly, trying to keep the drips of hair dye at bay. We talked about all this so many times when I first came to live here. Every option, every possibility was examined in forensic detail, detective style. There were only a few conclusions to be drawn:

1. Something bad had happened to my mum; an accident or a sudden illness or an act of violence, and she was dead and never coming back.
2. She'd run away to build a new life for herself, leaving me behind.
3. She'd had some kind of mental breakdown and been locked up in a high-security hospital, and she couldn't get out.
4. She'd had an accident that had left her with severe amnesia, and she had no memory of me at all.

Every one of those options had seemed too painful, too cruel to believe, so I'd pushed them away, packed them in a box and sealed it shut, shoving the box to the back of my mind. Somehow, writing songs has opened up the box again, let the hurt seep out. Having my picture in the paper has fooled me into hoping, dreaming that things could still be different.

'I try so hard, Bex,' I whisper. 'I always have. Why is it never enough?'

260

My foster sister wipes my tears with a wad of loo roll and scrubs away a smudge of crimson hair dye that has appeared at my throat.

'Lexie, don't,' she says. 'You are the best person I know, little sister, OK? The smartest, the kindest. You are amazing. The way you rescue everybody and everything – boxes of maps and sheet music, old toys, Mary Shelley . . .'

The little tortoise blinks up at us, head tilted to one side.

'And people too,' Bex pushes on. 'Me, Happi and now the whole gang of us in the band . . . even Marley. I don't think anyone would put up with that boy but you. I've got no clue what's eating him, but, trust me, he's more messed up than the rest of us put together . . .'

I sit down on the edge of the bath, feeling shaky, and Bex puts an arm round my shoulder.

She sighs. 'Thing is – I stopped being a detective years ago, but you never did, Lexie. You're still searching for . . . well, the impossible!'

'D'you think I'm crazy?' I ask. 'Ridiculous? Sad?'

'None of those things,' Bex tells me. 'OK, I tease you sometimes, but I love what you're doing, bringing people together. You're a rescuer, Lexie. You always have been, ever since I've known you. You find the lost stuff. People, pets, whatever. The thing is, I have a feeling that the person who really needs rescuing is . . . you.'

I wipe the tears away and try to smile. 'I don't think anyone out there is planning to rescue me,' I say. 'Too bad, huh?'

Bex shrugs. 'I don't know. I think maybe it's something you have to do for yourself.'

That doesn't seem fair. A wave of grief rises up inside me, angry, messy grief that threatens to pull me apart all over again.

'What if . . . what if my mum is out there somewhere, Bex?' I whisper. 'Looking for me?'

'Then she'll find you, Lexie,' Bex says. 'Or . . . not.'

I love Bex for her honesty, most of the time, but not today. Not today.

Lost and Found

Once I was lost without a map,
I cried but made no sound.
Once I was lost without a map,
But I turned it all around.

Chorus: If I was lost, would you find me?
If I was low, would you lift me high?
If I needed you, would you be there?
Would you even try?

The world looked clean and clear and bright,
The path was right ahead.
But then you came and all was changed.
I followed where you led.

Chorus

Into the fog, into the night,
The darkness everywhere...
I followed in your footsteps but
You were never there.

Chorus

27

Cutting It Fine

'I knew you could do it,' Marley says, pulling out his earbuds after listening to the GarageBand link I've just sent him. 'Cutting it fine, though, Lexie, cutting it fine! Another sad song . . . but brilliant. Just tell me it's not about me!'

We are sitting in the Leaping Llama, sharing a strawberry milkshake. I'm too tired, too weary now to tiptoe around his feelings, or to disguise my own. I go down the honesty route – Bex would be proud.

'It's mostly about my mum,' I tell him. 'She left me when I was nine . . . went missing, I suppose. I never found out what happened to her. That's why I'm in foster.'

264

Marley blinks. 'God, Lexie, I'm sorry – I had no idea!'

'You never asked,' I say with a shrug. 'All that time hanging out, talking about music and the band, plotting our rise to fame . . . you never asked.'

Marley frowns. 'But we can talk about anything!' he says. 'Lexie, I've never dated anyone else for more than a fortnight – only you. I thought you felt the same?'

'I like you,' I say. 'I like you a lot – you're one of my best friends. You drive me mad sometimes, but I still care – a lot. It's just I feel like we're more mates than girlfriend/boyfriend. You must feel it too, surely?'

Marley looks stricken, and I feel a stab of guilt. What if I've got this all wrong, if he's just shy or ultra polite or trying to take things slow? None of those things seem very Marley, though. I smile at the thought.

Marley is leaning forward, taking my hands in his. 'I've messed up,' he admits. 'It's a skill I have, everybody says so. And the last few weeks have been hectic for everyone . . . I've had so much on my mind I can't think straight. I just want this gig to go well. I've been rubbish, I know, but I'll make it up to you. Let's just get Saturday out of the way first, OK?'

I bite my lip.

'OK,' I tell him. 'Deal.'

Cutting it fine proves to be something of an understatement with the new song, but we are more skilled, more professional now, and we set to work once more, determined to whip it into shape.

We practise 'Lost and Found' night after night until we're ready to drop, until I am sure that Bex is about to smash her bass guitar over Marley's head, until I sense that Happi would like to stab him with her violin bow, until every last one of us wishes we'd never even dreamed of being a band. We're exhausted, but at least the end is in sight.

Millford is almost ready to protest, ready to party. The *Gazette* has published a final spread about the festival, showcasing the cool activities on offer and bringing the world up to speed on Ked Wilder. Apparently he has been off the radar for a decade or more, living quietly in the Devon countryside; nobody has been able to tempt him to pick up his guitar again until now. He's going to sing, he's going to speak out about the libraries and then he's going to give a TV interview about it all.

'Miss Walker says it's the BBC,' Bex says. 'How cool would that be?'

'Cool,' I say, but what I mean is terrifying. National TV. As in, TV seen by people outside Millford, outside the Midlands. People everywhere.

'Someone told Marley and he's gone even more power-crazy and perfectionist than usual,' Bex comments, fluffing up her newly crimson hair. 'Nightmare! The sooner this is over, the better.'

We watch the park transform, invaded by trucks and vans and teams of workmen who construct the main stage and mixing desk, put up a big backstage tent and four long marquees, then cordon off the whole thing with fancy festival fencing. I can't quite imagine that by Saturday the park will be rammed with people, people who want to support the libraries, who want to see Ked Wilder play – but it's happening. It's unstoppable now.

Marley crosses another day off the calendar, and another and another until finally we reach Friday, the day before the gig, and there are no more days to cross off. The new song is sounding pure and powerful, with a heart-stopping trumpet solo from Lee, soulful strings and some really intricate harmonies when Marley sings too. It's great, but Marley pushes us onwards, striving for some elusive perfection only he can see. The mood of the band is simmering somewhere just below boiling point. There is mutiny in the air.

'We're almost there,' Marley promises. 'Once more through the whole set and we'll have it sounding sweet as honey. From the top!'

But Sasha sits down heavily on the sofa edge, her shoulders slumped.

'I can't,' she says. 'I'm worn out and my head is hurting. Let's call it a day!'

'No pain, no gain,' Marley warns. 'Just once more through. Come on!'

'We've been here since four, Marley,' Bex says. 'It's past nine. Sasha's right. Enough is enough!'

'I reckon the timings were off on "Back Then",' Marley argues. 'Let's just get that sorted and then we can go!'

Soumia, always quiet, dependable, easy-going, shakes her head. 'Don't you ever listen, Marley? We tell you we've had enough and you don't hear us; you don't care. We're OK – we're good, even. As ready as we'll ever be. I've turned up to every practice – do you even know how hard that has been for me? The lies I've had to tell my parents? They think I'm at some kind of study club at school, or at Sasha's house, revising. I've had GCSE exams since the middle of May, Marley . . . I'm Year Eleven, remember? I sat three of the things this week and there are another two next week . . . but all you care about is this stupid festival tomorrow, and whether you'll make the big time based on our hard work. Well, sorry, I'm done!'

Soumia grabs her jacket and heads for the door, Sasha not far behind.

'OK, OK,' Marley is yelling. 'We'll leave it. Whatever. Don't walk out, Soumia – we need you! And Sasha – please!'

'Leave it, Marley,' Sasha says. 'Tomorrow is our big day – we need some sleep! I'll be back at ten for a last rehearsal, sure, and Soumia too – but right now we're going!'

The door clatters shut behind them.

'Sometimes you push them too far,' Dylan says into the silence. 'Chill out, dude. We're only human!'

We clear away in awkward silence, and the others leave in twos and threes until it's just me and Marley left. 'Sasha's

269

right,' I tell him. 'We all need some sleep. Things'll look better in the morning.'

'Will they?'

'Sure! They always do!' I promise, although I'm not sure that's actually true. 'C'mon, Marley. Let's lock up.'

We hide the key in its usual place underneath the steps and walk hand in hand across the park. It looks alien in the falling light, filled with the looming shapes of tents and marquees, and Marley can't relax. He's all wound up, convinced that Sasha and Soumia have walked out for good, that tomorrow's performance will be a disaster.

'They'll be there,' I tell him. 'They're just tired . . . They've had enough for today. We all have.'

'Am I the only person who actually cares about tomorrow?' Marley growls. 'Without me, the band would still sound like a car crash. Don't they get that it takes hard work and lots of practice to pull a set like this together? Is it wrong to be a perfectionist?'

'Marley, I . . .'

My voice trails away into silence as I notice a couple of figures up ahead of us in the half-light, close to the Music Zone tent. One of them is Sharleen Scott, dressed to kill in

270

tiny denim shorts and a crop top; the other is her boyfriend, six foot tall and built like a tank. Tank Boy turns, catches sight of Marley and instantly stands taller, gritting his teeth.

I feel cold all over. 'Ignore them, Marley,' I whisper. 'Just keep walking . . .'

But Marley has stopped in his tracks. His hackles are up, his eyes alight as he shifts from one foot to the other, his hands scrunched into fists.

'All right, loser?' Marley says calmly, clearly. 'Nice evening. Out for a walk with your dog?'

Sharleen's face slides from happy to horrified to hurt. She bursts into tears and her boyfriend launches himself at Marley, shoving him to the ground. All I can hear then is swearing and the crunch of knuckle against bone, grunts of pain and ragged gasps for breath – and Sharleen's sobbing in the background. Marley's face is slick with blood and dirt; he isn't even trying to fight back.

Cutting through the falling dusk sounds my own piercing scream.

'Help! Somebody, please help!'

28

The Lost Boy

Sharleen and her boyfriend run away, and I drag Marley to his feet. It's quicker to head back to Greystones than to try to get to Marley's house. We walk slowly because he's shaken and wobbly and I feel sick and shocked.

'Why did you do that?' I ask as we walk. 'Say that? You were horrible! I know Sharleen's a bully, but what you called her . . . there was no need, Marley. You asked for that fight. You made it happen!'

He just shrugs. 'Don't make me feel any worse than I do,' he mutters, and I am silent again, exasperated. I know how wound up he's been, and whenever Marley gets close to breaking point it ends this way. He looks for someone

273

bigger and meaner than he is and then launches into a fight that can only end one way.

As we approach the railway carriage, I let go of Marley for a moment to unlock the door. He sways a little, holding his ribs, then follows me inside, slumping down on to one of the bench seats as I fill the kettle and soak a clean cloth in hot water. In the light of the old railway carriage, I can see that his right eye is bruised and swollen, his cheek grazed. By tomorrow, he's going to have a pretty spectacular shiner. The timing could not be worse.

'Why d'you do it?' I ask him as I wipe the blood from his face. 'It's like a compulsion – the bruises from last time have only just gone. We talked about this, how it could mess everything up for the band. You genuinely picked that fight out of thin air, Marley. I don't get it!'

'I'm not a coward,' he says, wincing as I try to bathe his eye. 'If someone hits me, I'll hit them back – even if they're bigger than me. I'm not scared of anyone. Not even my dad.'

I frown, perching on the sofa beside him. 'Does . . . does your dad hit you?' I ask.

274

'Used to,' Marley answers. 'My mum, Dylan, me – but mostly me. Think he just hated me more than he hated the others . . . I don't know.'

Silence falls around us, ugly, awkward. For weeks I've been aware that Marley was holding back, showing me just a tiny slice of who he is. Now I know why.

He takes a deep breath. 'He doesn't hit me any more. He's banged up – in prison. They were after him already for fraud, but he hurt me so badly they did him for grievous bodily harm too. He went down for three years, and when he comes out he's not allowed to come anywhere near us. Now you know. Are you sorry you asked?'

'Not sorry,' I whisper. 'Oh, Marley . . .'

He shakes his head, distant, as if dredging up more memories.

'I want to tell you all of it, Lexie,' he whispers. 'I've never told anyone before, never met anyone I thought would understand, but you . . . maybe you will?'

'Tell me,' I say.

Marley frowns. 'D'you remember when you said you felt like we were more best friends than girlfriend/boyfriend? Well, that's a part of it. I'm no good at relationships. I don't

275

find it hard to actually get a girlfriend, but things never last. I know I have a bad reputation . . .'

'It's OK,' I whisper, but it's not OK, obviously. It's not OK at all.

'D'you want to know why he hit me, Lexie, that last time?' Marley demands. 'My dad? He caught me kissing someone from school and he was so angry, so disgusted, he tried to beat the badness out of me. He put me in hospital.'

'Oh, God!'

Marley takes a ragged breath in, raking a bloodied hand through his fringe. His eyes brim with tears, as if dragging up the past hurts more than his ruined face.

'D'you understand what I'm telling you, Lexie? D'you know what I'm saying?'

'Yes – your dad caught you kissing some girl from school . . .'

He shakes his head, shoulders slumped, silent for a long moment.

'No, Lexie, not a girl,' he tells me softly at last. 'I wasn't kissing . . . a girl. Do you hear what I'm saying? Do you get it now?'

My eyes open wide. 'I don't . . . but . . . what?' I murmur. 'Is this a joke?'

'It's not a joke. I – I think I might be gay, Lexie,' Marley is saying. 'Please don't hate me! Do you see now why my dad hated me so much? Why I hate myself? Why things between you and me got kind of weird?'

I've stopped listening, though. A dozen mismatched jigsaw pieces fall into place. The boy who's dated half the girls in the school but never stuck with anyone for long; the boy with a reputation as a user; the boy who's living a lie, who's been lying to me from the moment we met.

I feel sick, dizzy, as if I might faint.

'I'm no good, Lexie,' he is saying, distraught. 'I'm messed up, damaged, rubbish, just like my dad says, and if I end up in scraps sometimes and come off worst – well, I guess I deserve it . . .'

A surge of anger washes over me like an icy tidal wave, taking my breath away. I stand up, my whole body shaking.

'Are you asking for my sympathy?' I say. 'Seriously? When you've been lying to me all this time; playing games with my head? You told me I was different, that you'd never felt this way!'

277

'I haven't – you are!' he protests. 'I thought that maybe this time things might work out. I've tried so hard . . .'

But no matter how hard he's tried, Marley cannot bear to touch me. No matter how much he cares, I'm not enough. I'm not wanted, not needed . . . all over again. The taste of rejection is like ashes on my tongue. I slam out of the railway carriage, his voice echoing behind me.

I fumble my key into the lock of 3 Kenilworth Road and bolt up the stairs. Moments later, there's a knock on my bedroom door and I hear Mandy's voice asking if I'm OK.

'Not OK,' I croak. 'Please . . . leave me alone!'

But Mandy doesn't seem to hear because the door creaks open and she comes in anyway, sits down beside me on the bed. 'What's happened, Lexie?' she asks. 'Is it something to do with Marley? Has he . . . finished things?'

I laugh, but there's no humour, no joy in it. It's harsh and grating, a sad, ugly sound. Mandy puts an arm round my shoulder, gently. I want to move away, keep her at arm's length the way I always have, but suddenly I'm so weary of it all. I need someone to talk to, someone like a mother, and Mandy is here. She cares.

278

'It's over between me and Marley,' I choke out. 'But it's not what you think – it's worse. He doesn't want me at all; he never did. He's . . . he's gay!'

I tell the whole story – the mutinous rehearsal, the fight, the confession.

'Oh, sweetheart,' Mandy says. 'I'm sorry. That must be so hard for you to take in. You liked him so much . . . your first boyfriend. But it's good he's found the courage to tell you, Lexie. He must be a very mixed-up, messed-up boy right now – very lost – but I think he's trying to be honest, trying not to hurt you.'

'He's failed then,' I whisper. 'It feels like he's smashed my heart to bits. What's wrong with me, Mandy? Why can't anybody love me? Why do they always walk away?'

Mandy sighs, wiping my tears away with a tissue, stroking my hair. She is so close I can feel the tickle of her wavy hair against my cheek, breathe in the smell of her citrus shampoo. Somehow, quietly and without me even noticing, Mandy has become more familiar to me than my own mum.

'Lots of people love you, Lexie,' she is saying. 'Me and Jon, Bex, your friends . . . You are an amazing girl. You

279

really are. I think Marley cares a lot about you . . . It sounds as though he's just coming to terms with things himself. It won't have been easy for him.'

'No, but . . . it hurts!'

'I know, Lexie, I know . . .'

I don't want to feel sorry for Marley, don't want to understand. Right now, I just feel humiliated, foolish, rejected. Rejected all over again. Mandy seems to know just what I'm thinking.

'Lexie . . . we never talk about your mum, but maybe it's time we did,' she says softly. 'I think she loved you very much. We don't know what happened or why she vanished, and that's tough. Perhaps she had no choice, somehow, but even if she did . . . maybe she believed you'd have a better life without her. I am certain of one thing, Lexie. If your mum is out there somewhere, if she is . . . well, she will never stop loving you.'

'If she loves me so much, why isn't she here?' I yell. I push Mandy away, stumble across the bedroom to the window, as if by looking out at the starry sky I might somehow find some answers. 'Why didn't she care enough to stick around? I hate her, Mandy! I hate what she's put

280

me through. All these years, sick with guilt, thinking it was my fault . . .'

'It was never your fault,' Mandy says. 'Never, not for one moment. You were nine years old!'

'But she didn't love me enough to stay,' I murmur, and then the tears come again and Mandy's arms are round me, holding me tight. It's like a floodgate has opened; all the stress and pressure of the last few weeks, the hopes and dreams smashed into pieces, the nightmares . . . all of it comes out. I'm crying for me and I'm crying for Marley and I'm crying for the little girl I used to be, the girl who lost her mum and blamed herself, carried that blame for way too long. Maybe it's time to put that burden down, to stop searching, stop writing, stop hoping?

Maybe it's time to let go at last of the woman who let go of me.

Dear Mum,

I'm trying not to blame you. I'm trying to understand, but right now I am very, very angry.

I'm angry that you didn't take your tablets and let yourself get sick again. I'm angry that you were so selfish, yet made me feel I was the selfish one. I'm angry that you dumped me, left me in a corner like unwanted luggage. I'm angry that you didn't love me enough to stay.

I'm angry that I've kept Mandy and Jon at arm's length all this time, in case you came back and thought I was disloyal. I don't think you are coming back any more. I'm not even sure that I want you to. I do, but . . . like I said, I am angry.

I know that you were sick, and I am trying to understand.

I might not write for a while.

Love,
Lexie x

29

New Day

I wake at dawn, the first fingers of light pushing through the curtains to signal a new day. My eyes feel gritty from last night's tears, but my head is clearer than it's been for a while and, although my heart is hurting, my shoulders feel light, as if someone has lifted a heavy weight away.

When I check my mobile, there are a dozen unread messages from Marley, anguished apologies, pleas, despair. He spent the night at the old railway carriage, it seems, too scared to go home.

Stay where you are, I text. **I'll be there by seven.**

I shower, dry my hair, pull on my clothes for the gig, stuff my tambourine in a bag. I have no idea if we'll be playing now, not with Marley's face all bruised and swollen, but I'm determined we'll do our best.

Downstairs, Mandy is in the kitchen making coffee. I put my arms round her in a hug and hope she knows how much I love her, how grateful I am, how lucky I feel to have her and Jon and Bex to be my sort of family. I think she does.

'You're up early,' she says. 'How do you feel? How did you sleep?'

'Better than I have in ages,' I tell her. 'I'm going to talk to Marley. You're right – he was brave to tell me. He hasn't told anyone else, and he must be feeling awful about how I reacted. I need to put it right.'

'Good girl,' Mandy says.

I grab a cereal bar and head out of the house, Mandy huddled in her dressing gown on the doorstep, waving until I'm out of sight.

I walk through the park, the dew staining my red Converse. Already, vans and trailers are driving across the grass to their pitches ready to set up food and merchandise stalls. A team of festival officials in hi-vis jackets are directing everything and, as this is a free festival for those attending,

I wonder just how out of pocket Louisa Winter will be by the end of it all.

If we do manage to save the libraries, a lot of it will be down to her.

As I walk though the wild garden at Greystones, I see Marley, sitting on the steps of the old railway carriage, his head in his hands. He looks up as I approach, and I see that his right eye has swollen shut, an ugly purple-black bruise mottled around it. I flinch.

'I'm sorry,' he says at once. 'I'm so, so sorry. About everything. You have every right to hate me . . .'

'I don't,' I promise, sinking down on to the steps beside him. 'I could never hate you, Marley.'

'I'm a disaster,' he says, head in hands. 'I hate myself, if that's any consolation. But you need to know that I didn't mean to hide stuff from you – it's more that I've been hiding it from myself. I've been in denial ever since what happened with Dad . . .'

'Does anybody else know?' I ask, and he shakes his head.

'Nobody – not even Mum or Dylan. Dad was so ashamed of me he didn't tell a soul, not even in court. I suppose I should be grateful.'

'Grateful?' I echo. 'No, Marley. Your dad must have had his own fears and prejudices about this to lash out so badly, but what he did was very, very wrong. He made you feel like a piece of dirt just for liking boys instead of girls. You've been carrying this big secret for too long – it's eating away at you!'

Marley lets out a ragged sigh.

'There is nothing wrong with you,' I tell him softly. 'No matter what your dad told you, no matter what he did. You know that, don't you? It's OK to feel the way you do. It's not a crime, or anything to be ashamed of. I wish things were different, but I'm on your side, Marley, I promise.'

He takes my hand, holds it tight.

'I kept thinking that if I just found the right girl, everything would be OK,' he explains. 'I thought – I really did – that with you everything would be different, but it doesn't matter how hard I try . . . I'm still rubbish inside, just like my dad said . . .'

'Not rubbish,' I tell him sternly. 'Never. Crazy boy with death-wish tendencies and a slave-driver streak yes . . . but that's why we love you! From a personal point of view I wish things were different, but at least I understand now why things were so clunky between us.

'We'll figure this out together, I promise you. I think you should tell people; your mum and Dylan, the guys in the band. Maybe not now, if you're not ready, but some time soon, OK?'

Marley pulls me in for a gentle hug. There is no buzz, no passion – there never has been, I realize, but me and Marley are still friends. That's all that matters.

'OK,' I say. 'Right now we need to work out what to do about your eye and your ribs . . . and the gig.'

'Nothing you can do,' Marley says. 'I've blown it. Today I was going to meet Ked Wilder, maybe get us all a chance at the big time. All that hard work and I'm the one to wreck it all. The others are going to hate me for that!'

I roll my eyes.

'Ditch the self-pity, Marley,' I say briskly. 'We don't have time for that. Nobody's going to hate you, and the show will most definitely go on. There's too much at stake – the libraries, and the band, everything. Don't worry – I'm good at rescues . . . Leave this to me!'

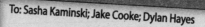

Urgent – please come to the railway carriage as soon as you can, will explain all but I need your help. Sasha, can you bring make-up? Dylan, can you bring Marley's stage clothes? Jake, just come down, fast as you can.

♥ Lexie x

30

Pirates

By the time Sasha and Dylan get to the old railway carriage, Marley has already gone up to the house with Jake, who promises he'll make sure Marley showers, washes his hair and eats some breakfast. 'We bumped into Sharleen's boyfriend again in the park last night,' I told Jake. 'Let's just say things didn't pan out well – we need a miracle here.'

'Don't panic,' Jake said. 'I'm on it.'

I tell Sasha and Dylan the same edited version of events; Dylan is not impressed.

'What's wrong with him?' the youngest Bob brother growls. 'I knew he was in trouble when he didn't come home . . . but today of all days!'

Sasha just opens up her make-up case on the counter. There are more pots and tubes and brushes of colour than I have seen outside an art room.

'It's what I want to do when I leave school,' she explains. 'If the singing doesn't work out, obviously! How bad is it?'

'Bad,' I tell her. 'The eye's pretty much swollen shut. Jake is going to try putting a bag of frozen peas on it, but I don't think anything will make it go away in time for the gig.'

'Are his hands are OK?' Dylan checks. 'He can still play? Still sing? Maybe we can stand him at the back?'

'Maybe. Or brush his fringe down, or make him wear an eye patch . . .'

'That might work,' Sasha says. 'An eye patch like a pirate? You can get away with all kinds on stage, can't you? What if we throw the odd striped T-shirt and bandana into the mix? It wouldn't be so very far from our black-and-red theme, and nobody'd think twice about the eye patch then!'

I grin. 'Sasha . . . you might just be a genius! OK – stripy T-shirts and bandanas . . . I'll start ringing round!'

By ten o'clock, when the others start arriving, half of them clutching random stripy T-shirts, Marley is sitting on

290

the railway carriage sofa with a bag of frozen peas held to his face.

'No shouting today,' he promises as the others pile in. 'My head hurts too much. I'm sorry I got so wound up last night. You were right, Soumia. All of you. I was stressed and strung out. I was being an idiot. It's a skill I have.'

'I was just so tired,' Soumia says sadly. 'I'm sorry too.'

With good relations restored, Sasha sets to work tweaking things so that everyone has a touch of pirate style: a red spotted bandana here, a stripy top there, and we are good to go. Sasha tries a big black felt pirate hat belonging to her little brother on Marley, but everyone decides it's too distracting for the lead guitarist, so Dylan gets it instead.

Little clumps of players start up: George, Happi and Romy going over the string sections, Bex and Dylan working on the bass, Lee playing random trumpet solos just for fun. Weaving through it all, Sasha goes from person to person checking make-up – a cool pirate girl in a red dress with added petticoats, her blonde hair backcombed to within an inch of its life and tied up with a spotted bandana. George gets a cartoon fake moustache, Lee and Dylan a swipe of cheeky Jack Sparrow eyeliner. Romy looks so different, older and more confident. Even Bex submits to the paintbox and brushes and emerges looking the fiercest pirate of all.

As for Marley, he seems a whole lot better than he had first thing. Showered and fed, with homeopathic arnica cream gently rubbed into his face and ribs as prescribed by Jake's mum, he looks like he just walked off the set of *Pirates of the Caribbean* in his striped top and skinny jeans and bandana and pirate patch. You can't see the black eye at all; nobody would even guess it was there.

'OK,' he says. 'Thanks to Lexie, Sasha, Jake and my long-suffering little brother, the crisis has been averted. We're back on track, a bit behind schedule but still in the game, and that's what matters. There's time for one more run-through of the set before we have to head over to the park for our soundcheck, so get ready . . .'

He hands something small and jangly to Jake, who takes it, looking puzzled.

'OK,' he adds. 'A last-minute addition to the line-up. Jake's going to be playing triangle, as he promised all those weeks ago. You've been amazing behind the scenes, Jake, we couldn't have done without you – but all the tech stuff

292

is taken care of for today's gig and I didn't want you to miss out on the limelight. So . . . anyone got a spare stripy top for Jake? Your little sister gave me the triangle, so I know you've been practising!'

Jake groans and tries to wriggle out of it, but he's outvoted.

'OK – the whole set, once more, from the top . . .'

Lee's ear-splitting trumpet call erupts, and we're off.

Here we go!

Love,
     Lexie x

31

Hold On

An hour later, we're down at the park, wearing our 'artist' ribbon wristbands and scoping out the main stage. The area in front of the stage is still fenced off because the main events don't begin until two, but even so it looks daunting. In a little while we'll be up there, soundchecking, then playing for real. It doesn't seem possible, somehow.

The festival is packed already. Little kids are tripping about dressed as Alice in Wonderland or Harry Potter or Little Red Riding Hood, and families are lining up to take pictures with the big painted character boards that have sprung up all around the park, poking their faces through the cut-out holes and morphing suddenly into Peter Rabbit or the Famous Five or Wimpy Kid. A slinky green dragon is snaking about through the crowds, and someone dressed as Willy Wonka is handing out golden tickets that turn out to be forms to sign up for a library card.

The librarians are in costume too: the grey-haired assistant from Bridge Street has transformed into a very convincing Beatrix Potter and others disguised as Dumbledore, the Gruffalo and Angelina Ballerina are lurking by the Book Zone tent where a blackboard advertises storytelling at set times throughout the day. Right now, a queue of teens is building up for the Rae Kelly event (Bex has to grit her teeth and look away) and a crowd of excited middle-aged women are clutching books to be signed after listening to a talk by bestselling author Miranda Marsh, an old friend of Louisa Winter. Boo McLay and Joshua Chikelu are doing events too, and a TV camera crew are filming a pop-up poetry slam as we pass by.

'The telly!' Marley says, and I nod, half wired and half terrified at the thought.

Outside the Fun Zone tent, students from the local art college are working with kids to paint a huge image of the BFG, and we are careful to give the Music Zone a wide berth when we hear the whiny, grating voice of Sharleen Scott screeching out over the loudspeakers. Whoever is in charge must think the same as we do because the volume is reduced abruptly. The others exchange glances, but I cannot find it in me to hate Sharleen Scott now; I've seen her crying, vulnerable. I think that underneath the tough-girl veneer she is as lost as any of us.

'Mandy and Jon will be here soon,' Bex reminds me. 'With Jon's friends from Yorkshire and Mandy's mum and her friend. If you think this is busy, think again – it's just the start.'

'My parents are here already,' Sasha says. 'No pressure then!'

'I hope mine don't show,' Soumia comments. 'They don't know I'm doing this. They think I quit the band weeks ago, when they told me I couldn't do that photo shoot at the library. If word gets out, I'm in big trouble . . .'

'No way,' Sasha says. 'You should have said! Let's hope they don't find out . . .'

I check my mobile for the hundredth time.

'OK, time to go,' I say to Marley. 'Are you OK?'

He squeezes my hand. 'Better than OK, thanks to you,' he says. 'I'm good. Let's do this thing!'

Heading backstage feels slightly surreal, as if we've sneaked in illegally to stalk Ked Wilder. We are treated like professionals by the sound crew, trekking up on to the stage to set out our instruments and work out placings. It has already been agreed that Dylan will use the drum kit from Ked Wilder's backing band, to make the transition easier and because it's about a million times better than his own battered kit. He sits down behind it and runs through a few beats, his face lit up with the thrill of it.

When the sound crew realize that we've never played in public before and don't actually know what we're doing, they're kinder than you'd expect, asking all the right questions and helping us to spread out across the stage in a way that makes sense both visually and musically. Unexpectedly, I'm at the front, sharing a mic with Romy and Happi; Marley, Sasha and Bex are right up there too. George is happier sitting further back, and parks his stool and cello near Soumia's keyboard, while Lee and Sami settle for a space near the drums. Jake, terrified he'll mess up, tries to hide in a corner, but Marley tells him there's

298

nothing much he can get wrong with only a triangle to play. 'Mime, if you're worried,' he says.

We run through 'Back Then' a couple of times so the sound guys can check the levels, and it must sound OK because the crew are grinning now, giving us the thumbs-up sign. 'Nice vibe,' one of them tells us, and when everything is checked, and everyone is happy, they tell us to relax in the Green Room while they soundcheck Ked Wilder.

'Why is the artists' waiting area called the Green Room?' Marley wonders as we approach the backstage tent. 'It's not green, not even a room . . .'

'It's all to do with the colour your face is going to turn as the nerves kick in,' Bex tells him, and he sticks his tongue out at her.

We flash our wristbands and go inside. The buffet table is piled high with sandwiches, fruit and chocolate. Bottles of fizzy water and cartons of orange juice are crammed into ice buckets to cool.

'Wow,' Sasha says. 'Is this real?'

'It's definitely real, and I think we should eat,' Dylan says. 'Some of us had to skip breakfast, thanks to my annoying brother!'

299

I take a paper plate and collect a few bits to nibble. I'm too nervous to relax. Two o'clock is bearing down on us like a runaway train, and it's terrifying.

I spot Miss Walker with Joshua Chikelu and Rae Kelly, and Bex runs over to meet Rae and have a brief fangirl moment. Two older women wander in: one turns out to be a famous TV actress, and the other is the author Miranda Marsh.

Then Louisa Winter sweeps in with Ked Wilder, and we're wide-eyed and speechless in the presence of this sixties pop legend, tall and stringy and much older than the pictures in the newspaper would have us believe. He's still dressed time-warp style, as if he's just stepped out of a boutique on London's Carnaby Street, in mirrored shades, skinny black jeans, a turtleneck sweater and winklepicker boots. He has a black suede fringed jacket slung casually over one shoulder, and the same moptop haircut he wore in the sixties. It looks slightly odd on a man who must be in his seventies, but I have to admit he looks like a star.

He and Louisa have made today possible, called on friends, courted publicity, cashed in favours – even dipped

300

into their own pockets to stage this festival. All for the libraries, and all because they believe that people don't have to sit back and let bad things happen.

'Children!' Louisa Winter calls out, waving. 'Oh, let me look at you – yes, I am loving the styling! Clever! Are you excited?'

We fall over ourselves to tell her just how excited we are, how thankful for the opportunity, how grateful for her help, but she just laughs.

'Oh, you'll be brilliant, I'm certain of it,' she says. 'My good friend Ked here has been looking forward to meeting you! Ked, I've had you to myself all morning and you're probably sick of the nostalgia trip. Stay here with the kids and relax a minute. I'll get us something to drink . . .'

Louisa wanders away and we swarm around Ked, shaking hands, babbling compliments, telling him how thrilled we are to be his support act.

'I'm probably your biggest fan,' Marley gushes, barely able to stand still. 'I've read your biography – from the library, of course – and I've tried to model myself on you. Music is my life! I'm ambitious, I'm determined . . . I really want to get to the top!'

'You certainly sound like a younger version of me,' Ked responds, laughing. 'I was probably a little full-on, back then. I've learned to slow down, but still, I have to admire that youthful enthusiasm!'

Ked Wilder pushes his mirrored shades back on his head and without them he looks less starry, more like someone's granddad dressed up for a fancy-dress party.

'We write our own songs,' Marley rushes on. 'All originals – Lexie and I work in partnership, then build up the arrangements as a team. We have a big line-up because we wanted a full, rich sound . . . something powerful, something different. I think you're going to like it!'

'I'm sure I will,' Ked Wilder says. 'I'm looking forward to hearing you play . . . This is your first big gig, right?'

'First *ever* gig,' I blurt out. 'I think we're all terrified!'

Ked Wilder just laughs. 'If you weren't a little bit scared, you wouldn't be human,' he tells us. 'Just channel that energy and pour it into the music. Here's a tip – when you're up on that stage, act like you belong there. Believe that the audience are there just for you and play them the best bloomin' set they've ever heard. Blow 'em away!'

302

Then Louisa Winter is back with two glasses of champagne she's conjured from somewhere, and a photographer appears and starts taking shots of us with Ked Wilder, and before we know it one of the sound guys appears and tells us it's time. Romy's face is white with fear and George looks clammy and sick – and Marley looks so hyped I think he might explode. I lean in for a hug, avoiding his ribs.

'Thank you,' he whispers. 'For everything, Lexie. Let's go and be awesome!'

'I'll be in the wings to watch you,' Ked Wilder says, and Miss Winter squeezes my hand and tells us she'll be introducing us, and I'm so high I think I'll either fly or faint – I can't tell which.

We all walk outside together, and we can hear the crowd, see that the space around the stage that was empty earlier is now overflowing. My limbs seem to have turned to water.

Miss Winter strides on to the stage, a small, fierce figure in crumpled jade silk, the red hair streaked with white and bound up with twisted jade and turquoise scarves that trail down her back like pennants. The crowd stills as she takes the mic and welcomes everyone to the festival.

'We've never had a festival in Millford before,' she

303

announces. 'Thank you all so much for coming along to support the libraries and to see my good friend Ked Wilder play his first live gig in over a decade. Ked spent a lot of time here back in the sixties, and he loved reading. A lot of his musical inspiration came from books, and a lot of his books came from libraries!'

'This festival was Ked Wilder's idea, and shortly we'll be hearing him play, but right now I want you to listen to a group of young people who care so passionately about the library cuts that they have been at the very heart of this protest. These young people are not just campaigners; they are musicians too. Please give a warm Millford welcome to brand-new teen talents . . . the Lost & Found!'

There's a roar of applause as we walk on stage, but I'm shaking so hard the tambourine rattles in my hands and Happi has to take my elbow and march me over to our shared mic. I look round at the others. George is biting his lip, Jake winks at me, and Romy looks as if she might cry; Sami just nods in my direction, his eyes storm-dark, still wearing his threadbare coat in spite of the warm day, in spite of the promise he made to Marley. I can't help smiling, and he smiles back.

304

Then Marley steps forward to his mic, and the last of my fears fall away.

'Hello, Millford!' he yells. 'It is a privilege to be here today to share our music with you! We'd like to say a huge thank you to the wonderful Louisa Winter and the legendary Ked Wilder, as well as all the everyday heroes who run our brilliant libraries and work so hard to keep them open. Without them, this festival would not be happening . . . and we wouldn't be here!

'We are the Lost & Found, and we're a new band, barely two months old. All our songs are original and this is the very first time we've played in front of an audience, so be kind! Our first song is called 'Back Then'. Take it away!'

Lee's trumpet blasts out the intro and the others come in one by one, and by the time Sasha starts to sing I'm not shaking any more – I'm dancing, leaning into the mic with Romy to sing the harmonies. When the last chords die away the applause begins, and that's when I know that all the hard work was worth it, that Marley was right all along when he said we had something special, something different.

It flies by way too fast. People do not walk away – they keep coming, leaving the sideshows and stalls and tents to

 305

come and listen. I can't help wondering if somewhere out there, my mum might be watching, listening, but the thought lifts away just as quickly when I catch sight of Mandy and Jon down at the front, crammed right next to the stage, arms waving, faces shining with pride.

When we come to the end of our last track, 'Library Song', everyone goes crazy. Cameras flash and people shout for more. We could do a dozen encores if we wanted to, but we only have five songs.

'Thank you, Millford!' Marley yells into the mic. 'You have been the best audience ever. I hope you liked our songs – and I hope you like our message for Millford Council. *Save our libraries!*'

The crowd roar their approval and start chanting for an encore again.

'Always leave them wanting more,' Marley says as we run offstage, and I think by then we all want more. We all see Marley's vision of what we have, what we might achieve. We hug each other, laughing and crying, standing in the wings as Ked Wilder stalks onstage and the crowd go crazy.

We are so high it feels like the world is at our feet, like anything is possible.

For a long time after you left, I thought you were watching me, looking out for me. I'm not sure I believe that now. But if you're out there, Mum, even if you're looking down from the stars . . . I hope you're proud.

Love,
Lexie x

32

Afterwards

Afterwards, I remember the moment when Marley took my hand and tugged me away from the wings, down the steps to the front of the stage, the others following. We wriggled our way into the crowd, found Mandy and Jon and the others, and Sasha's parents, and Lee's, and a whole lot of other people too. We laughed and danced and sang along with the words of Ked Wilder songs we didn't even know we knew. I remember how brilliant it was, how the air crackled with hope and our hearts filled up with the joyful music of a lost generation.

I danced with my friends, with Bex and Happi and Marley and all the kids from the Lost & Found, and I loved every moment.

Later on, a snippet of Ked Wilder's first scheduled performance in a decade makes it on to the six o'clock news.

'I don't perform much in public these days,' he tells the camera. 'But Millford's libraries matter – they're the reason I'm doing this.'

'Wow,' Mandy says. 'I think your library campaign just got its best plug yet! And if he's still doing that documentary interview with the BBC, that'll help too!'

On Sunday, four or five different newspapers mention the story – one with a big colour picture of Marley and me with Ked Wilder and Louisa Winter, and a huge headline: 'Sixties Star Mentors Talented Teen Band in Bid to Save Libraries'. The report claims that Ked Wilder was really impressed with our set and hopes to see us soar to success.

'How about that?' Marley crows. 'Fame and fortune at last!

Two days later, the council announce that they've changed their mind about the libraries. We watch the U-turn on *Reporting Midlands*: one of the Men in Suits stands in front of the Library Love Letters display in Bridge Street Library and tells the camera that their decision is nothing to do with the letters, or the festival, or the rallies and petitions and outpourings of support. Nothing at all to do with any of that.

'Libraries have always been an essential part of Millford society,' the council spokesman says. 'Closing them was a last resort. That's what the general public don't seem to understand. While all this nonsense was going on, we've been working very hard behind the scenes to create a plan that will allow us to go forward into the twenty-first century with a modern, comprehensive and cutting-edge service . . .'

'What does that even mean?' I wonder out loud.

'I don't know,' Bex says. 'But how dare he call our campaign nonsense? There's no way they'd have budged on those closures if we hadn't kicked up a fuss!'

'We won,' I remind her. 'Even if the council are sore losers, we still won!'

'We did,' Bex agrees. 'Shouldn't we be celebrating?'

'Let's go to the library!' I say, and so we do, all of us – me, Bex, the rest of the band, even Mandy and Jon. When we get there we discover we weren't the only ones with the idea – Bridge Street Library is packed with people, and Miss Walker is jubilant, swishing about in a new dress printed with pages from *Alice in Wonderland*, her face shining. She hugs us all, wiping her eyes, and I know that whatever happens with the band, we have achieved something special, something important here. It all turns into an impromptu party, with the Lost & Found playing our second ever gig between the bookshelves. Someone raids the CD shelves and plays Ked Wilder on Miss Walker's tinny little CD player, and we party on until midnight because *we* saved the libraries and we're proud of it, no matter what the council may say.

Not all the fallout from the festival is good, alas.

Soumia's parents have found out that she's been lying to them about the band, and they're furious. They'd told her to drop it weeks ago; she'd only managed to keep coming by pretending she was at a GCSE study group on practice nights. 'There's no reasoning with them,' she tells us. 'I'm grounded, forever most likely . . . no more band. I'm sorry.'

Looks like we'll be needing a new keyboard player.

It all feels a bit sad, a bit weird, and when my social worker Josie calls to arrange a meeting in a coffee shop in town things get weirder still. It's not the Leaping Llama – Josie's not the hipster type – just a quiet department store cafe, but it feels strange because I don't see Josie much these days, and when I do she usually just calls over to the house.

'What's it about?' I ask Mandy and Jon as they drop me in town. 'Nothing I should be worried about?'

'Of course not,' Mandy says, but she looks anxious all the same.

'Can't you come with me?'

'Not this time,' Jon tells me. 'But we'll be waiting. If you need us, just call, OK? We're here for you, Lexie. Always.'

When I walk into the cafe, I spot Josie straight away – she's sitting at a table with Louisa Winter, sipping tea. A glass of orange juice, my drink of choice back when I was nine, sits waiting for me, but I frown because the picture doesn't quite add up. Josie and Louisa Winter do not belong together. They stand up to greet me, and Louisa puts her arms round me and hugs me, telling me that Ked Wilder hasn't stopped talking about us since the festival.

 312

'He says that if there's anything he can do to help you, or help the band, you just have to say the word.'

'Wow!' I say. 'Tell him thank you!'

'Is that what this is all about?' I ask, sitting down awkwardly. 'The festival? Ked Wilder?'

Josie frowns. 'In a roundabout way, perhaps it is,' she says. 'You've been making quite a stir lately, Lexie Lawlor. And a few days ago Miss Winter here called me with some information that could make even more of a stir . . .'

Louisa puts her teacup down, clasps her hands together. I can see faint traces of blue paint around her fingernails.

'Do you remember the very first time we met, Lexie?' she asks me. 'You were with Jake, and I asked you if we'd met before because you reminded me of somebody?'

'Vaguely,' I say.

'I remembered who it was, eventually,' she tells me. 'It was a young girl called Janine Howard, the daughter of a very dear friend. She was the image of you – right down to the haircut – when she was your age. I knew Janine well; she had quite a stormy time of it later on – met a boy her parents disapproved of, dabbled in drugs . . . I think there were some mental health issues too, but they didn't realize

313

that until later. At one point, her father threw her out and the two of them stayed in the old railway carriage for a week or so . . .'

I feel very still, very scared. My heart is beating hard and I can't quite seem to find my breath. My eyes close and I remember the first time I saw the railway-carriage bedroom, the smashed glass of the dressing table, the heavy, sad feeling that filled the air.

'The two of them ran away eventually, and my friend has never quite recovered from it,' Louisa Winter goes on. 'She lost her only daughter . . . never heard from her again. Can you imagine?'

The question hangs in the air. I can imagine, of course. I can imagine very well what it feels like to lose someone you love . . . I've lived it, after all.

'I now know that you've been through something very similar,' Louisa says. 'The thing is, Lexie – on Monday, my good friend Alexandra Howard called me. She'd seen the photograph of you and me with Marley and Ked, in the *Sunday Report*, and she wanted to know who you were. You looked so like Janine, you see! And I told her that your name was Lexie Lawlor, that you were thirteen years old . . .

314

and in foster care, according to young Jake. Alexandra called the social services right away.'

I can't think straight, can't understand. My mouth is too dry for words, but when I reach for the orange juice my hand shakes so much I knock the glass over and Louisa grabs napkins from a nearby table to mop up the spill.

'Are – are you saying you've found my mum?' I whisper.

Louisa takes my hand. 'No, Lexie, not your mum,' she says, calm and steady as always. 'Your grandparents, Alexandra and Tom Howard. And they really want to meet you!'

I shake my head. 'But . . . I don't get it!' I argue. 'My mum was called Nina Lawlor, and she told me her parents were dead!'

'Nina was a nickname from when she was little,' Josie tells me. 'And Lawlor was your dad's surname – she must have adopted it. Her parents weren't dead and they never stopped missing her. Nina came back to Millford in the end; perhaps she had it in her mind to make contact with her parents, let you meet them? We don't know, because, for whatever reason, that didn't happen. Alexandra and Tom had no idea they had a granddaughter!'

'I don't . . . what happens now?' I ask.

315

'Nothing too dramatic,' Josie reassures me. 'We have a lot of sorting out to do, a lot of planning. You're settled with Mandy and Jon, so we won't be moving you for the moment – or at all, unless you want us to – but we thought you would want to meet your grandparents. They lost their daughter and you lost your mum, and nothing has changed that, but now you have each other!'

Josie taps away at her mobile phone, and then looks across the cafe expectantly. I follow her gaze to where a middle-aged couple have just walked in. The woman is like an older, more conventional version of Mum; the man is gruff, smartly dressed, wary.

I stand up, shakily, wiping hot tears from my eyes, and the couple walk towards me.

Marley and me are sitting on the steps outside the old railway carriage a few days later.

'I can't believe it!' he says, laughing out loud. 'Ked Wilder has the music world in the palm of his hand, and he's offering to be our mentor!'

'Um . . . mentor?' I echo. 'That's not quite what he said! Don't believe everything you read in the papers!'

 316

'Near enough,' Marley crows. 'He likes our stuff and he wants to help us in any way he can. How cool is that? A bright future for the Lost & Found, saved libraries, unexpected grandparents . . . things are looking up!'

'It's the end of us two, though,' I point out sadly. 'Just friends from now on.'

'Best friends, though,' he tells me. 'And, Lexie, trust me – this isn't the end, not really. It's just the beginning . . .'

Dear Mum,

The boyfriend thing didn't work out, but we're still good mates, so that's OK. There's someone else I think I like, but I'm not sure anything will come of it. I'm talking to Mandy about all that kind of stuff now, and she's great – I think you'd be happy I have people like Mandy and Jon looking out for me. I hope so. I really do.

We ended up getting in the papers again, and on TV . . . because of Ked Wilder, I guess, and saving the libraries and stuff. I've spent weeks hoping that you'd see my picture or spot me on TV, but in the end it was my grandparents who saw the pictures. They got in touch with social services and, although I'm still getting to know them, they seem nice. I wish I'd known they existed before . . . I might not have felt so alone.

I still have so many questions, Mum, but I don't know if I'll ever find the answers. I've carried so much hurt around for so long now, and I have to let go and get on with my life, even if I never do find out what really happened to you.

Maybe some things are just meant to stay a mystery.

I love you to the moon and back.

Love,
Lexie x

PS I don't think I'll be writing again, Mum, but I will never forget you, I promise.

Read on for a extract from this gorgeous new story by Cathy!

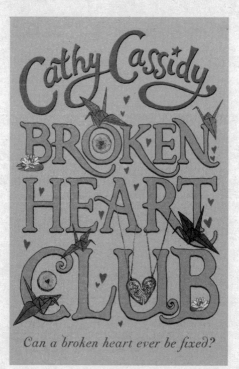

Andie, Eden, Ryan, Tasha and Hasmita love being part of the Heart Club. They've promised to stay best friends forever and nothing can tear them apart. But sometimes things happen that you couldn't ever have expected and forever might not be as long as you think . . .

Prologue

It's a Friday afternoon in late July, the summer after Year Six, and Andie and I are scrabbling about in the drizzle, wrestling with the canvas of the big old bell tent and giggling too much to actually get anywhere. Ryan from next door comes over to put up his little pop-up one-man tent and we drag him in to help, but that makes things worse because Andie is too busy flirting to take much notice of ropes and canvas. In the end Ryan goes home and Andie's dad has to untangle the mess and help us put the tent up properly.

It's Andie's eleventh birthday, and we've planned a sleepover party, a garden camp-out for the Heart Club. It's also a bit of a farewell thing, because Tasha and her family are moving to France in ten days time and Hasmita will be going to a different secondary school after the holidays. Tomorrow Andie and her family are going to Scotland for a week's holiday, so even if Tasha's family are still here by the time she gets back, it could be the last time we all get together properly. I get a sick feeling in the pit of my stomach at the idea of us being parted.

We all know that things are changing, and none of us like it.

'It's got to be a sleepover to remember, Eden!' Andie says, peering out at me from under her anorak hood. 'It's got to be special!'

'It will be.' I promise, because our sleepovers always are and who cares if the TV says this is the wettest summer we've had in forty years? A bit of rain can't stop the Heart Club from having fun. We spread bright rugs, pillows and blankets inside the bell tent, hang battery-powered fairy lights around the inside, make raggedy bunting to liven up the inside of the tent by tying endless strips of bright fabric scraps on to the strings of fairy light. They look beautiful, in a frayed and slightly frantic way.

'OK,' Andie declares at last. 'It's my birthday, and I reckon we've earned cake. C'mon, Eden, let's go get ready – the others will be here soon!'

We head for Andie's bedroom, a tiny boxroom painted sunshine yellow and papered with boy-band posters and bright, manga-style paintings she's done herself. Andie's mum is saving the birthday cake for later when Hasmita, Tasha and Ryan arrive for the sleepover, but she's given us jam tarts and cheese on toast, and Andie ramps the music up to full volume to get us in the mood.

'I think I'm in love,' Andie says, throwing her arms wide. 'Ryan Kelly. Who knew?'

'Isn't it a bit awkward falling in love with one of your best friends?' I ask.

'It's awesome, because we've known each other forever,' she says. 'We already love each other in a friend-ish way, I just have get Ryan to see I'm not just the girl-next-door. Imagine . . . all this time and I've only just noticed how cute he is!'

I smile, but I know my ears have gone pink and I hope Andie doesn't notice.

'Tonight could be the night,' Andie sighs. 'He might say something – make a move. Or maybe I will! What d'you think?'

'Cool . . . why not?' I say, even though it's not cool and I can think of a million reasons why not. It doesn't matter, though; I don't think Andie will do anything more than flutter her eyelashes at Ryan. She's eleven; she's not ready for romance yet – any more than I am.

For me, friendship comes first anyway; I think it always will.

I reach into my sleepover rucksack, pull out a little parcel wrapped in gold tissue paper and tied with red raffia, and hold it out to Andie.

'Just wanted to give you this before the others get here,' I say, grinning. 'Happy birthday, Andie!'

'Oooh! What is it? It's tiny . . . but heavy!'

She peels the tissue paper back and lifts out a little silver heart pendant, the kind that breaks in two so that two best friends can share. Her face lights up with glee, and she holds one half of the heart pendant out to me.

'Wow! I've always wanted one of these!' she exclaims. 'Thank you. A friendship locket, right? One half for me and one for you, because you are the best, best friend ever, Eden Banks. I love you loads, and I'll always be there for you, promise!'

I believe her. Andie has always been there for me, even through this past year. My parents split up, and I don't think I could have got through it without Andie's support.

'Any word from your dad?' she asks, as if reading my mind.

'Nothing,' I tell her. 'I think he's forgotten me.'

'Oh, Eden,' Andie says. 'As if anyone could ever do that!'

She puts on her half of the heart pendant while I put on mine, and then she flings her arms around me and hugs me tight, laughing, and I can smell the vanilla scent of her shower gel all mixed up with the aroma of strawberry jam and cheese on toast.

'I love my pressie,' she tells me. 'I'm going to wear it always. Awww . . . tonight is going to be epic!'

Epic is one word for the camp-out, I guess. By midnight, the rain is sheeting down and the bell tent is full of puddles; Ryan's little one-man tent has already collapsed in a soggy heap.

It's like the end of the world, but Andie doesn't do failed sleepovers and somehow she makes it all seem cool, an adventure. We eat hot pizza with pineapple chunks and chocolate birthday cake with ice cream. Ryan has brought over his copy of *Harry Potter and the Philosopher's Stone*, which he wants to lend to Andie, but she's not in the mood to listen to chunks of story right now. She has swiped her mum's iPod and makes us all sing karaoke to dodgy, ancient cheese-pop. By the time Ryan launches into his rendition of 'It's Raining Men', we're laughing so much the tears run down our cheeks, and it doesn't matter any more about the leaky tent or the fact that fate is pulling us apart.

Andie ramps up the volume to max, opens the tent flaps and drags us out into the downpour.

'Noooooo!' Tasha is screeching. 'I'm soaked already! Are you crazy, Andie Carson?'

'I'd rather be crazy than boring,' Andie declares, pulling me and Tash out into the deluge. 'C'mon, guys, think of it as a rain dance in reverse! Who cares about a little bit of rain? Once you're wet, you're wet, right?'

'A little bit of rain?' Hasmita argues, pushing her black plaits up into a woolly hat with a grin. 'Trust you to look on the bright side, Andie! This is a monsoon, a tsunami, a hurricane . . . plus it's pitch black! Are you serious?'

'Andie's never serious,' Ryan says. 'But I am – get dancing!'

He flings himself into a full-on disco routine, playing it for laughs, and the rest of us join in, half-hearted at first and then with energy. I'm drenched, but it feels awesome, like I am truly alive for the first time in forever. I'm wearing pyjamas and a rain jacket, my feet soaked and squelching in thick socks that are already slick with mud. Trickles of cold rain slither down my upstretched arms, but I'm laughing, singing, loving every moment. I'm with my best friends. So what if it's chucking it down? We are the Heart Club, and not even the wettest summer in forty years can stop us having fun.

I'm dancing around, my arms wide like wings, doing some kind of shimmy with Andie when I slip on a patch of mud, twisting my right ankle. I gasp with pain. Andie whirls away from me in the dark, oblivious, her bare feet sliding in the wet grass, long fair hair transformed into rat's-tail ringlets flying out around her face. Tasha and Hasmita dance on too, faces turned up to the starless sky . . . they have no idea I've hurt myself. Only Ryan sees me stumble, and drops his comedy routine to come over and help.

'You OK, Eden?' he asks, and like an idiot I am blushing because he's noticed and cares.

I try shifting my weight on to the damaged foot, and red-hot pain sears through me instantly. 'Ouch,' I say. 'I can't stand on it . . .'

Ryan takes my elbow and steers me back to the tent, and I crawl inside, peeling down one squelching sock. He flicks a torch on, and in the little pool of yellow light I can see my ankle is already swelling, looking disturbingly spongy and Swiss roll-like.

A surge of self-pity rolls over me. My ankle is throbbing and sharp, shooting pains make my eyes brim with tears. The party vibe has ebbed away; I am soaked to the skin, cold to the bone.

'I've spoiled everything,' I say. 'Our last proper get together ever, and now it's ruined . . .'

'Hey,' Ryan argues. 'Nothing's ruined – this was just an accident, OK? Dancing on wet grass in torrential rain probably isn't the greatest idea ever!'

'But . . . things are changing,' I protest. 'Everything's being shaken up. What if we break up, drift apart?'

'Shhh,' he says, softly. 'Change isn't always a bad thing. And nothing is going to come between us, Eden, OK? I promise.'

The words seem laden with meaning. I feel my cheeks flame and there is a fluttering in my chest that's halfway between terror and joy. It's all in my imagination, of course . . . Ryan is talking about all of us, not just me and him.

But then his fingers curl around mine, and I don't pull away. I have never held hands with a boy before. I have never felt so happy, or so scared.

'You're shivering,' he says, grabbing a blanket to drape

around my shoulders. The tip of one finger wipes the tears from my eyes, and then he leans over as if he might kiss me and I panic and turn my face away, and he kisses my ear. I think I might die of happiness.

The music ends, and there is a sudden shift in the air around me. I open my eyes to see Andie kneeling in the doorway of the tent, her face frozen, eyes like ice. An Arctic chill falls over me.

'She slipped,' Ryan is saying. 'A twisted ankle, pretty bad. I was just . . .'

He trails away into silence.

'You were just what, Ryan?' Andie asks, her voice clipped and cool. 'Getting in the way, most likely. I'll sort this. You'd better ring home, Eden, get them to fetch you. You might need an X-ray or something. Too bad.'

A new track begins to blare out of the iPod speakers, an upbeat number about it being the end of the world as we know it.

I think maybe it really is.

Catch all the latest
news and gossip from

Cathy Cassidy

at

www.cathycassidy.com

✦ Sneaky peeks at new titles

✦ Details of signings and events near you

✦ Audio extracts and interviews with Cathy

✦ Post your messages and pictures

Don't Miss a Word!

Sign up to receive a FREE email newsletter
from Cathy in your inbox every month!
Go to *www.cathycassidy.com*